Stephanie

Other Books by Jack Weyland

Stephanie

JACK WEYLAND

Deseret Book Company
Salt Lake City, Utah

No part of this book may be reproduced in any
form or by any means without permission in writing
from the publisher, Deseret Book Company,
P.O. Box 30178, Salt Lake City, Utah 84130.
Deseret Book is a registered trademark of
Deseret Book Company.

First printing March 1989
Second printing July 1989

Library of Congress Cataloging-in-Publication Data

Weyland, Jack, 1940-
    Stephanie / by Jack Weyland.
      p. cm.
    Summary: Reluctant to admit her addiction to alcohol and drugs,
sixteen-year-old Stephanie finds it impossible to give up drinking
and pills until she faces her problems in a hospital treatment
program.
    ISBN 0-87579-203-0
    [1. Alcoholism—Fiction. 2. Drug abuse—Fiction. 3. Mormons—
Fiction. 4. Conduct of life—Fiction.] I. Title.
PZ7.W538St 1989
[Fic]—dc19   88-37541
                               CIP

My thanks to the three families who have assisted me in the preparation of this book. They each have gone through the experience of having a chemically dependent son or daughter. Their combined experiences form the basis of Stephanie.

1

It was a perfect night for a keg party. An afternoon rain had left behind clear sky and the smell of pine.

Most of the twenty people there Stephanie knew from high school, but one was a stranger. He moved with the easy confidence of an athlete. Several times she caught him staring at her. She was used to that, of course—her red hair worn stylishly short, her wide-set blue eyes, her high cheekbones, the relaxed, fun-loving way she had with her friends—all made it impossible for anyone to ignore her. She didn't mind having him watch her, except that whenever she returned his gaze, he seemed embarrassed and looked away. And yet she could tell he wasn't the shy type.

Around ten o'clock he broke away from a group of football players he'd been talking to and started to cook a few hot dogs over the campfire.

She was by then both curious and hungry. She approached him as he knelt by the fire, cooking two hot dogs on a stick. He was of medium height, with blond hair and the kind of build that only people who lift weights ever acquire. When he turned his head, she could see each set of muscles act as it came their turn. And yet, in spite of what she generally thought about guys who went around trying to look macho, she was impressed, and that puzzled her even more. "Any chance I can have one of those?" she asked.

He didn't look up to see who was asking. "If I give you one, then everybody else'll want one too."

"Tell you what, I'll eat in the dark behind a bush so nobody'll notice."

He looked up, saw that it was her, and smiled. "Behind a bush? Hmmm . . . up a tree would be better."

She smiled back. "Up a tree's no problem for me."

He fixed a hot dog and handed it to her. She took a bite. "This tastes *so* good. It's the first real food I've had all day."

He fixed himself one, then turned to her. "Hey, aren't you supposed to be up a tree about now?"

She brushed back a few rebellious strands of hair. "Oh yeah, right. You're not going to hold me to that, are you?"

"Hey, the way I look at it, a deal's a deal." He took off his warm-up jacket. She wasn't sure if that meant he was warm or that he wanted to show off his muscles. He looked around for the biggest tree he could find. "How about that one over there, all the way to the top?"

She smiled. "Look, the hot dog wasn't that great. Actually I had to give it a seven—I took one point off for no relish and two off for ashes. It's definitely not worth killing myself over, which is what'll happen if I try to climb that stupid tree. Okay?"

He started pulling her toward the tree. "You're not afraid of a little hundred-foot vertical climb, are you?"

"No-no-no-no-no." She rattled the words off like a machine gun but it didn't do any good. "No! I mean it now! Stop!" Her protests weren't too convincing because she was giggling.

When they got to the tree, he asked, "Need any help to get you started?"

"Yeah, sure. How about if I stand on your face?"

"You're outrageous, you know that?" he said.

"Sure I know it. I also know you've been watching me all night."

"You wish," he scoffed.

"Man, you are such a liar—you know you have. I've got a question though—how come I had to be the one to make the first move?"

He shrugged his shoulders. "I wasn't sure getting to know you would be worth it. See, the thing is, I like my women smart, not just smart looking."

"You mean they got to be as smart as you?"

"Yeah, right."

"No problem. The only thing around here that isn't as smart as you is that fence post."

He turned to look. "Which fence post is that?"

"The one on the left there. The one on the right is fairly intelligent."

He shook his head and gave her a big grin. "All right, you win. I surrender. Do you take prisoners?"

She shook her head. "Not usually."

"How about making an exception?"

"I'll think about it."

They stood there looking at each other. Gazing into his brown eyes made her feel as if he was someone who could be trusted. But it was his smile that got to her most of all. It was a nice-guy, hometown-goodness kind of smile. And yet there was something in it that was also slightly mischievous. It was the kind of smile a boy gives his mother when she's caught him having ice cream for breakfast.

There was, however, one thing about him that amused her—his after-shave. He'd put way too much on. For some reason it made her glad to know that even a guy like him sometimes felt a little insecure.

He broke into a big easy grin. "This is fun, isn't it?"

"Yeah, really. Flirting should be an Olympic event."

"If it was, you'd get a gold medal for sure. What's your name?"

"Stephanie Bradshaw. And yours?"

"Craig Miller."

"How come I don't know you?" she asked. "What year are you?"

"I graduated last year."

"From Stevens?"

"No, Central."

"Central? Are you serious? What are you doing here?"

"I came with Bucky Stevens."

"How do you know Bucky?"

"Every time Stevens and Central played each other in football, whenever I carried the ball Bucky tried to rip my head off."

She smiled. "Yeah, well, I can see how that'd build a friendship all right."

"What year are you?" he asked.

"I'll be a senior next fall."

"Who did you come with?"

"Jessica Phillips."

He smiled. "Oh yeah? I thought you might've come with a guy."

"Not tonight."

"That's good news for me then, right?"

"Not really. About the only thing you've got going for you now is that you can cook hot dogs over a fire. Where'd you learn?"

"I'd rather not say."

"C'mon."

"Promise you won't tell?"

"Hey, trust me."

"When I was a kid, I used to be a Boy Scout."

"Hey, everybody! Craig here is a Boy—" He put his hand over her mouth but she broke away, chanting, "Craig is a Boy Scout, Craig is a Boy Scout . . ."

4

He reached out to grab her, but she slipped away and ran into the woods. "You might as well give yourself up," he called out. "We have the place surrounded."

In the darkness she felt a rush of excitement. It was like being a kid again and playing hide-and-seek—except this time she wanted to be caught.

"You can run, but you can't hide," he yelled, starting after her.

She turned and bumped into a tree, spilling beer on her jean jacket. It made her mad but she didn't want to stop their game. She found a path that headed up through the trees. At first it was hard to see, but then her eyes adjusted to the dark. Sometimes she made noise just so he wouldn't lose her.

Finally she stopped on top of a ridge and waited for him to catch up. She could hear the muffled voices of her friends down below and see the smoke drifting up from the campfire. And she could hear him coming closer.

When he reached the top, she stepped out from the tree where she'd been hiding. "Looking for someone?"

"Yes, ma'am, I'm searching for a desperado named Stephanie."

"What did she do, rob a bank? Kill somebody?"

"I'm afraid it's much worse than that."

A look of horror crossed her face. "Oh no! You don't mean—"

"Yes, ma'am, she made fun of a Boy Scout."

"How awful!"

"It's pretty serious, all right. I have a description of her in case you see her out here in the woods. By the way, what are you, a lumberjack?"

"Why, yes, I am," she answered. "But how did you know?"

"Because of the woodchips stuck in your cheek. Well, anyway, here's the official description. She's got the most awesome red hair. She's the kind of girl you never forget.

To strangers she's got this look, like, 'Hey, there's nothing you can do to impress me.' But once you get on her good side, it's like sitting by a warm fire on a cold night. Never try to put her down, though, 'cause if you do she'll come back at you with some comment that'll wipe you out every time. I mean, it's a real challenge to talk to this girl. . . . Uh, let's see, what else? Oh, yeah, her eyes are unbelievable. I mean, to look in her eyes is like being taken over by an alien life force."

" 'Alien life force'? If you talk to other girls this way, you must be the loneliest guy in the world. I'm serious."

"You want to sit down and talk some more?"

They went to a large slab of rock and sat down. She looked up at the sky. "There must be a million stars out there tonight."

"Just a minute, I'll check it out. One, two, three . . . "

"Are all guys from Central like you? If they are, I'm transferring Monday. I'm serious. The guys at Stevens are such jerks."

"Don't bother me, I'm counting. Seven, eight, nine . . . ten . . . "

"Gosh, Craig, you can count to ten. That's really good. You've worked a long time on that, haven't you!"

He put his hands out like he was going to choke her. "They say nobody can hear you scream out here in the forest."

"Yeah, like I'm really scared. Tell me something. Has anyone ever said you look like Tom Cruise?"

"No."

"That's because you don't. Just kidding—you do, kind of. I know, it's your smile." She paused. "You got a cigarette?"

"Sorry."

"No problem. I'll get one from somebody once we go back." She looked up. " 'Star light, star bright, first star I see tonight. Wish I may, wish I might, have the wish I wish tonight.' "

"I've got my wish," he said.

"What's that?"

"I'm here with you. Just you and me and the stars."

She mimicked his deep voice. " 'Just you and me and the stars, babe.' "

"I'm serious. I've been wanting to meet you all night."

"So why didn't you come over and start talking to me?"

"I figured you'd think I was just another guy out cruising for girls."

"Oh, and you're not?" she teased.

"Not really. But after I got here, I couldn't stop looking at you. You're so terrific."

"Sometimes I feel like that, but most of the time I don't."

"What about tonight?"

"Tonight I can take on the world. Of course, a few beers always does that to me, but that's what's so great about drinking, right?"

"You don't need to get confidence from a bottle. You've already got everything going for you."

"Yeah, sure, if you say so." She paused. "Not to change the subject, but are you going to kiss me before we start back?"

"Do you want me to?" he asked.

She felt a little foolish. "Well, yeah . . . but, you know, I don't want to beg or anything. It's up to you."

It was the kind of kiss she'd always dreamed about — tender, gentle, and lasting so long that they broke apart only when they absolutely had to breathe again or they would die.

"Not bad," she said softly. "I give it a nine point five. I had to take half a point off because . . . because . . . gosh, I can't remember now. Let's try it one more time. Maybe the reason'll come back to me."

7

Suddenly he got up and walked a few feet away and stood there with his back to her.

"Is something wrong?" she asked.

"No, not really."

"C'mon, Craig, tell me what's wrong."

He turned around. "It's just that we don't know each other very well."

"Not well enough to be kissing, you mean."

"Yeah, right."

She tried to turn it into a joke. "Just my luck, right? Two thousand single guys in this town — and I get one with a conscience."

He didn't laugh, and that made her feel even worse. "Sorry, I didn't mean that. Actually I'm impressed. Most guys aren't like you. I feel like such a fool. Guess I got a little carried away there, huh? Sorry. How about if we just chalk it up to your after-shave."

"What about my after-shave?"

"What is it, industrial strength? Do you buy it in fifty-gallon drums?"

He smiled and then she smiled and suddenly things were fun again.

"Look, you're absolutely right," she said. "We should get better acquainted. Tell me something about you and then I'll tell you something about me. We'll make a little game out of it. You go first."

There was a long pause, and then he said, "I go to church every Sunday. It's an important part of my life."

"What church do you belong to?"

"I'm a Catholic. How about you? Are you very religious?"

"I used to be, but right now I'm trying to stay as far away as I can from religion."

"How come?"

"It's a long story. Look, how about if we go back and join the others? I'm dying for a cigarette and I need a drink

8

in the worst way. I spilled mine running away from you. Besides, now that our hot dogs have had a chance to digest, we'll probably drink everyone else under the table."

He smiled. "Yeah, sure, we'll become legends in our own time."

"Hey, I already am."

They started downhill. Before they got very far, they heard the sound of vehicles screeching to a stop. Then they saw flashing red lights appear near where their friends were. They heard someone with authority barking out orders, but they couldn't quite make out what he was saying.

"What's going on?" she asked.

"I think our little party has just been busted."

Somebody poured water on the campfire, making a thick cloud of steam and smoke. Then there was the sound of car doors slamming and vehicles starting. The flashing red lights moved away, and suddenly everything was swallowed up by the night and they were all alone and the forest was silent, dark, and deep.

David Bradshaw, Stephanie's father, was spending that Friday evening doing church work in his office at home. He was on the stake high council, and there were two things he needed to accomplish before he and his wife, Emily, left for San Francisco on Monday. First, he needed to prepare a sacrament meeting talk for Sunday. He would be visiting the ward in Belle Fourche, South Dakota, about an hour's drive from their home in Rapid City. Also, he needed to review the plans for Family Week, which the stake was sponsoring for Thanksgiving week. That night he wrote a letter to the governor, asking him to proclaim Thanksgiving week as South Dakota Family Week. It would be good public relations for the Church and might help reinforce in peoples' minds how family oriented the Mormons were.

He had a hard time trying to decide what to talk about

9

for sacrament meeting. He ended up choosing a topic he felt was important but one that was generally overlooked by the members in his stake. He would speak on the importance of keeping a journal.

After he finished preparing his talk, he decided he'd better set a good example and write in his own journal.

April 15

Last week after high council President Winder took me aside and told me how much the stake presidency appreciated the job I was doing. He said that I'm the one high councilor that most bishops request to speak in their wards. So maybe all my hard work is finally beginning to pay off.

Everything seems to be going fine with the family. We're all healthy. Stephanie seems a little more positive about getting involved in church activities. She's in the roadshow this year, so maybe that's a good sign.

Tomorrow Emily and I will get away for a few days. I'll be giving a paper at the San Francisco meeting and there are some other sessions I should attend, but, even so, I'm hopeful we'll be able to mix pleasure with business. Emily is talking about us renting a car and driving south to Monterey and Carmel. It all sounds good to me. We need a break. We won't have to worry about Stephanie and Kim because Emily's mother is coming to stay with them. I can hardly wait to go. Being department head has been so much more of a headache than I ever imagined.

Today Bill Stevens talked to me about applying for the position of vice-president. He said a lot of people on campus would support me if I was interested. I told him I'd have to think about it.

Emily, smelling of shampoo and bath oil, her dark brown hair tinted with occasional strands of gray, slipped quietly into the room. She came up behind David, put her hand on his shoulder, and leaned down and kissed him on the cheek.

He looked at her and smiled.

"It's Kim's bedtime," she said, "so is it okay if we have family prayer now?"

"Sure, I'm done here anyway." He closed his journal. "You smell nice."

"Thank you."

"You know, I wouldn't mind running off for a few days with a woman like you."

After eighteen years of marriage, their romantic games were still fun even if they were more subdued now. She smiled. "Is that so?"

"Yes, that's so. You're still the most wonderful woman I know." He put his arm around her shoulder, and together they started for the family room, where Kim was watching TV. "Where's Stephanie tonight?"

"Oh, she's just over at Jessica's watching a movie. She said she'll be in a little after midnight."

A minute later the three of them knelt down for family prayer. David asked Emily to offer it. Mostly she prayed for her family.

The woods were quiet except for the whispering of the wind through the trees.

"So what are we supposed to do now, gather nuts for the winter?" Stephanie asked, trying to make a joke of it, but unable to hide the fact she was worried.

Craig rested his hand on her arm. "Relax, it's no big deal. We'll walk to the highway and then hitchhike into town."

"What if nobody gives us a ride?"

"Then we'll walk all the way into town," he said.

They began walking slowly back down the trail. He led the way.

"My parents can't ever find out about me being here," she said.

"Why not?"

"They don't even know I drink," she said.

"Why haven't you told them?"

"Because they'd die if they ever found out," she said.

"How come? They drink, don't they?"

"Are you kidding?"

"Everybody drinks at least a little," he said.

"Not my parents. Not even a drop."

"Why not?"

"It's against their religion. I'm serious."

"What religion are they?"

"Mormon."

"Are you a Mormon too?" he asked.

She paused. "Well, yeah, sort of."

"How come you drink then?"

"Because it's fun. Besides, all my friends drink."

"When did you start?" he asked.

"When I was twelve. I was babysitting for this family and they had a liquor cabinet. After the kids went to sleep, I used to, you know, like, experiment. I remember thinking, hey, there's nothing to this. All my life people have been telling me that if I even took one drink, I'd go to hell or something. But after the first drink I knew it wasn't that big of a deal. And that's the way it's been with everything. I started using pot when I was fourteen. People in my church make it sound like you do pot one time and you'll end up out on the street selling your body for drugs. I'm serious. But really, it wasn't that big of a deal. I didn't even get high on it until the third or fourth time. And then it was just, you know, nice and mellow."

"What else have you tried?"

"Let's see—Valium, speed, ecstasy, Quaaludes. What about you? What have you done?"

"Just a few beers on the weekends. How do you pay for all this?"

"Well, a lot of times it doesn't cost me because I'm the life of the party."

"But you must have to pay for it sometime though."

"Well, yeah. Sometimes I use my mom's bank card."

"Doesn't she ever wonder where all her money is going?" he asked.

"Not really. Like, I make up school expenses. I think she's paid for a school annual about ten times this year. How did you get started drinking?"

"My dad gave me my first beer. It was at home around the kitchen table. I remember him saying, 'If you're going to drink, do it in front of us, and do it responsibly.' "

"I wish my dad was like that. Want to trade?"

"He's okay. We get along pretty good."

"Was he a football hero too, when he was your age?"

"Yeah, he was, in high school. He never went to college. I'll be the first one in the family to do that. I start in September."

"Where will you go?"

"St. Martin's College in Minnesota."

"A Catholic school, right?"

"Yeah."

"You've got your life pretty much all mapped out, don't you?"

"Anything wrong with that?"

"Not as long as you're the one doing it. In my case, my folks had my life planned out before I was even born. Go to Brigham Young University and then get married in the temple—that's all I've ever heard. But I figure I've pretty much trashed their plans for me by now. They just don't know it yet. But as long as I go to church, hey, everything's cool. They think they've got this perfect little angel daughter."

"You don't have much good to say about your church."

"If you let it, the Mormon church'll just take over your whole life. Like, if you ever watch an R-rated movie, they act like you're the worst person in the world. Or if you swear once in a while. Or even if you watch TV on Sundays.

My dad gets mad if I don't write in my goofball diary once a day. In my church, every time you turn around, there's somebody preaching against something. I just couldn't take it anymore."

"Why don't you quit your church?"

"I will someday, but I can't now because of my parents. Right now it's easier this way. They're happy and I'm happy."

"But you're living a lie, aren't you?"

"Yeah, I guess so, and it does get kind of crazy sometimes. I'll be so glad when I can move out and be on my own. But hey, next week is going to be fun. My mom and dad are leaving town for a few days. While they're gone, me and my friends from school'll be doing some major partying. Want to join us?"

"What about school!"

"Oh, we don't worry about school. We've got ourselves a system for that. How about it?"

"I work days," he said.

"Where at?"

"I work for my dad. He's a carpenter."

"What about after you finish for the day?"

"There's something else you need to know. I'm going with someone."

There was a long silence. She tried to hide her feelings. "Oh."

"Her name is Rachel."

"Is Rachel a good little Catholic?"

"Yes."

"How long have you been going with her?"

"Two years."

"Does Rachel know you're fooling around behind her back?"

"You're the first girl I've been with, other than her, for two years."

"So why aren't you with her tonight?"

14

"She's out of town. She's got an aunt who's sick, so she's watching her aunt's kids for a few days. I was going to stay home tonight, but Bucky called and talked me into coming with him."

Loose pebbles on the steepest part of the path forced them to proceed slowly in the dark.

"So I take it you won't be partying with me next week then, right?"

"No, probably not."

She hated to sound bitter, but she couldn't help it. "Well, I'll just have to try and get along without you. I'm sure that won't be too hard."

"Look, I'm sorry. I should've told you earlier."

"Why didn't you?"

"Because it was so much fun to be with you."

"Rachel's the real reason you were feeling so guilty about us up there, isn't it? I mean, it wasn't because of your noble principles so much, was it?"

"Yes, it was because of her. Look, I don't know if it's even possible, but I'd still like us to be friends."

"Rachel might not appreciate that."

"Probably not, but both her and my parents would. They're always telling us we shouldn't see so much of each other."

They stood before the steamy remains of what had once been their campfire, then started walking down the gravel road that led to the highway.

"How come Mormons don't drink?"

"We've got this thing called the Word of Wisdom that says don't drink or smoke or use coffee or tea."

"Other churches don't have that. How come yours does?"

"It has to do with Joseph Smith. He's the man who started the Mormon church."

He noticed a car coming toward them. "We'd better

get off the road in case the cops are coming back to look for us."

They hid in the trees. She leaned against him. He put his arm around her. She rested her head on his chest. His hand gently touched the top of her head and moved down along her hair to her neck. He did it several times. She loved his gentleness and wanted him to kiss her again, but she knew he wouldn't because of Rachel.

The car passed by.

"We can go now," he said softly.

"Why couldn't I have met you before Rachel did? I'm sorry. Forget I said that. That was so immature of me to say that. I don't know what's wrong with me. I guess I need a beer."

"Are you okay?"

"Yeah, sure, I'm okay."

They started walking again. "You were saying something about Joseph Smith. What made him decide to start a church?"

"When he was a boy he wanted to know what church to join, so he went into the woods and prayed about it."

"Did he get an answer?"

She almost didn't want to tell him. "Yeah."

"What was his answer?"

"God and Christ came down and told him not to join any church." Just talking about this made her feel uncomfortable.

"Yeah, right. Why'd they say that?"

"Look, I'm not exactly the best person to ask about this, okay?"

"All right, but you still haven't told me why Mormons don't drink."

"Another time God told Joseph Smith that drinking and smoking and coffee and tea weren't good for people."

"What do you mean God told him? You mean like face to face?"

"Yeah. The things God told him are written in a book."

"God doesn't just come down and talk to people anymore."

"Mormons believe he talks to a prophet."

"Is that what you believe?"

She sighed. "It doesn't matter anymore what I believe."

"Why not?" he asked.

"Because if you mess up one too many times, God just writes you off, and from then on it doesn't matter what you do because you're going to go to hell anyway. That's where I'm at now. So I try not to think about God and hope he doesn't think about me either. I mean, I don't want to be zapped, right?"

"It'd be better for you just to quit your church than to go sneaking around the way you do."

"Look, I'm doing the best I can, okay?" she said.

"I think you should get off drugs."

"I'm cutting down. Really I am. Besides, why do you care?"

"I want us to be friends," he said.

"Hey, you don't have to con me. I know you feel guilty about what happened tonight, so you're trying to make it be okay by pretending you want us to be friends. I know I'll never see you again, but hey, don't worry about it. I enjoyed it up there as much as you did. We had our little fun, but now it's over. It's no big deal. That's life."

They were still walking on the gravel road, pitted with bumps. Suddenly she stumbled. He grabbed her to keep her from falling. They continued walking. He reached out to hold her hand.

She pulled back. "No."

"Just in case one of us falls."

Having him hold her hand made it hard for her to stay mad.

They came to a place where the road crossed a stream. "Want a drink?"

"Me, drink water?" she joked. "No thanks."

He went down to the water's edge. She could hear him splashing.

"What are you doing?" she asked.

"Washing off the after-shave."

"Why?"

"You don't like it."

She went down to the stream where he was. He stood up, his face still wet. "Let me dry you off," she said.

"I can use my shirt."

"No, let me do it."

She undid her jacket, which was tied around her waist, and found a clean part and carefully wiped his face with it. She loved to touch his face even if it was through one layer of cloth. The silence was broken by the sound of crickets nearby and the soft bubbling of the creek. She put the jacket down and gently traced the outline of his face with her fingers, and then, sensing he was feeling guilty again because of Rachel, she suggested they continue on.

He helped her up the embankment and they started walking again. This time she reached for his hand.

"What's Rachel like?" she asked.

"She's kind of a serious person. Very religious. She keeps me in line pretty much. She's never dated anyone except me."

"How old is she?"

"She has another year of high school left, like you."

"And then what? Marriage?"

"I don't know. We've talked about it. Our parents want us to wait."

Finally they made it to the highway. After five cars went by, one stopped and picked them up and took them into town and dropped them off at Craig's house. When they got there, it was nearly midnight. "Can you wait here?" he said. "I'll go get my keys and be out in a minute, and then I'll give you a ride home."

She sat down on the lawn and looked at the house. It was a modest home. A pickup truck was in the driveway, as well as an older car. A minute later Craig came out and opened the car door for her. They started for her home. "I want to see you again," he said.

"Why?"

"I'm not sure why."

She smiled. "Good reason."

"I like being with you."

"You'd have to tell Rachel about me."

"I will just as soon as she gets back."

"I'll think about it."

"Also, can I look at the book that says what you believe God told Joseph Smith?"

"Yeah, sure."

A few minutes later he pulled in front of her house, which was dark except for an outside light. She asked him to wait a minute. She unlocked the front door, went upstairs to her room and got her triple combination, and came back to the car. "Here you are," she said.

"Thanks. I'll get it back to you in a few days. Oh, one other thing. You'd better not let your folks get a whiff of that jacket, or they'll know what you've been up to."

"Yeah, right. I'll hide it until I get a chance to wash it. See you. Thanks for everything."

She watched him drive away and then put the jacket in the trunk of her car and went inside.

As she passed her parents' bedroom, her mother called out.

She stuck her head inside the door. "Hi, Mom."

"You came in and then went out again? Why?"

"I loaned my triple combination to a guy I met tonight. We talked a lot about the Church. I think he's interested."

"That's good. Where were you tonight?"

"Jessica and I just had some people over to her house to watch a movie."

"Was her mother in the house with you?"
"Yeah, sure. Well, good night."
"Good night. Be sure and say your prayers."
"Yeah, sure, Mom, just like always."

2

The next day Stephanie slept late. At eleven o'clock her fifteen-year-old sister, Kim, came in. "Did you borrow my jean jacket last night?"

Stephanie barely opened her eyes. "Yeah, it's in the trunk of my car."

"Why'd you put it there?"

"I spilled beer on it. Sorry."

"I wish you'd ask before you just take my things," Kim said.

"You borrow my things all the time without asking."

"Not as much as you do."

"Look, it just needs to be washed is all. Can you do it for me so I can get some sleep?"

Kim paused. "All right."

"And while you're at it, how about washing the other stuff I was wearing last night. It's there on the floor."

Kim picked up Stephanie's dirty clothes, then said, "Jessica called last night after everyone else had gone to bed."

"What'd she want?"

"She wanted to know if you'd made it home okay. She said for you to call her first thing today."

"All right, I will, but right now I need to sleep, okay?"

"Don't forget there's a roadshow practice today at one."

She groaned. "How'd I ever let myself get talked into that anyway?"

"You can't back out on us now. Everyone's depending on you."

"All right. Wake me up in time to go."

There was silence in the room, but Stephanie hadn't heard Kim leave yet. She opened her eyes. Kim was staring at her.

"What's wrong?" Stephanie asked.

"What are you planning to do when Mom and Dad are gone?"

"Nothing special."

"You're going to ditch school and party all the time, aren't you."

"Well, one time maybe, but that's all."

"Don't, Stephanie. That stuff is no good for you."

"You're right. I'll cut down. Honest."

"You're always saying that but you never do."

"I will this time. You'll see. I've got to. I'll end up flunking every class if I don't shape up pretty soon."

"Did you have a good time last night?"

"It was okay. Oh, I met a guy."

"What's he like?"

"He looks like Tom Cruise. I'm serious. You should see him when he smiles. Let's see, what else? He graduated from Central last year, and he was a big football star so he's got a nice build. He's so much fun to be with. We had a terrific time together." She paused. "Just one thing — he's already going with someone."

"You'll take care of that soon enough."

"We'll see. Oh, another thing about last night — we got busted. They came and hauled everybody away. Luckily Craig and I were taking a walk so they missed us. We had to walk to the highway and then hitchhike into town."

"Lucky for you they didn't catch you."

"Yeah, right. But if they had, I would've told Mom and Dad that I was there but wasn't drinking."

"You think they'd believe that?"

"Sure, why not? They always believe what I tell 'em. Look, I'm really tired."

"I'll go."

"Oh, could you wash my tennis shoes too, in case I got beer on 'em? I'll do you a big favor one of these days."

Kim bent down and picked up the shoes and then left.

Emily Bradshaw spent Saturday morning preparing casseroles for next week. Even though her mother would be coming Sunday night to stay with the girls, she didn't want to burden her down with having to cook for everyone. Around eleven thirty she heard the mailman and went out to get the mail. She sat down and read a letter from her mother, confirming again when she would arrive by plane from Utah.

When Emily returned to the kitchen, she heard the washing machine going. She opened the door and called downstairs. "Who's doing a wash?"

"I am," Kim answered.

"Kim, I did your things yesterday."

"I know, but this is just a light load."

"We can't run the washer for just a few things. How many times have I told you girls that?" She went downstairs. Kim was standing there looking guilty. Emily opened the washer and looked at what was being washed. "These are mostly Stephanie's things, aren't they?"

"Yes, except for the jean jacket."

"Why are you doing Stephanie's wash?"

"She asked me to."

"You don't have to do everything she asks, do you?"

"Not really."

"Honestly—you doing this for her while she's up there

23

still sleeping. From now on, if Stephanie has things to be washed, you let her do it. We can't go around picking up after her all the time. If we do, she'll develop bad habits and end up driving her roommates at BYU crazy."

"All right."

"Why did she want her tennis shoes washed?"

"They must've got dirty, I guess."

"Well, don't you do this for her anymore."

"Okay."

Kim started up the stairs.

"Kim?"

"What?"

"Even though I'm not happy about you running the washing machine without a full load, I want you to know I think Stephanie is lucky to have you for a sister."

"Thanks, Mom."

Kim went to her room and closed the door and sat at her desk and did homework. She liked to do it on Saturday so she didn't have to worry about it on Sunday. At noon she went downstairs and made sandwiches and took one of them up to Stephanie's room. "It's time to get up," she said.

Stephanie barely opened her eyes. "Just a few more minutes."

"No, now. You'd better get going so you'll have time for your shower. Oh, I brought you a sandwich."

Stephanie sat up on the edge of the bed.

"I washed everything like you said," Kim said.

"Thanks."

"Mom got after me for running the washer with such a light load and also for doing your stuff."

"Yeah, sure."

When Kim left, Stephanie put on a white terry cloth robe and locked her bedroom door. Because she was the oldest, she got one of the two bedrooms in the house with its own bathroom. Her parents had the other private bathroom, which was reached through the master bedroom. The third bathroom on the second floor was down the hall. Kim used that one.

Lately this arrangement had become especially convenient for Stephanie.

With the door locked, Stephanie pulled out from the farthest corner of her closet a locked file box marked *Diary. Keep Out.* She used a key to open the file box, took out a plastic bag containing marijuana, cigarette paper, and matches, went into the bathroom, closed the door, rolled herself a joint over the sink, turned on the shower and the exhaust fan, but didn't get in the shower. She sat on the floor, her back resting against the wall, and lit up.

Ah, she thought as she inhaled deeply, now the day can begin.

After she finished this morning ritual, she took her shower.

The roadshow practice was a boring ordeal for Stephanie. She sat in the back of the gym waiting to be called to do her part, wishing she could go be with her real friends.

A girl she barely recognized came up to her. "I'm Tara Cramer. I'm the new Laurel class president. We missed you last Wednesday night."

Stephanie knew that if Tara hadn't been the Laurel class president, she never would have come up to her.

"I had to study." It was her standard answer for not being involved more in church activities.

"Well, maybe next time."

"Yeah, sure."

Stephanie wandered into the rest room. There was nobody else there. She stood in front of the mirror and brushed her hair, then looked down at the brush and noticed how much hair was in it. She had just cleaned it a few days ago. *What's going on?* she asked herself.

25

Kim came in. "They're calling for you."

"Look, why don't you take my part?"

"You do it. C'mon, this'll all be over before long."

"I know, but the whole thing is so stupid."

"Yeah, but with you in it, at least it has a chance. C'mon, help us out. We've got to beat Second Ward this year."

Stephanie was still looking at the clump of hair in her brush. "My stupid hair's all falling out."

"It's because of the way you've been living. You gotta quit."

"I will."

"When?"

"Real soon. I've got to take advantage of Mom and Dad being gone next week, and then that'll be my last time."

"I think you should give it up now. Today."

"No, not today, this is Saturday. The weekends are for partying, right? C'mon, let's go back."

After practice Stephanie drove to Jessica's house. Nobody answered the door. She let herself in and went to Jessica's bedroom. Jessica was still asleep. She could get away with sleeping so late because she was an only child and her mother was divorced and wasn't home much.

"Rise and shine!" Stephanie called out, opening the curtains to let in the light.

"Go away," Jessica moaned.

"C'mon, snap to it." She yanked the covers off the bed.

Jessica sat up. "Hey, woman, I see you made it home last night."

"Sure, no problem."

"Who was that guy you were with?"

"Craig Miller. He graduated from Central last year."

"It looked like you were both having fun. What'd you two do when you snuck away?"

26

"Nothing."

Jessica smiled. "Yeah, sure, like I really believe that."

"It's the truth. Besides, he's going with someone already. What'd the cops do to you guys last night?"

"It was the sheriff's office. They called our folks. My mom had to come down and get me."

"What'd she say?"

Jessica shrugged her shoulders. "She doesn't care. She says she drank when she was my age, so it's no big deal to her."

"What do you want to do tonight?" Stephanie asked.

"I met a guy from Tech a couple of days ago. He told me about a party tonight." She smiled. "You know what they say, college guys are more fun. You interested?"

"Sure, why not?"

"What do you want to do now?" Jessica asked.

"I dunno. Have a few beers, I guess."

"Who with?"

"Just ourselves."

"I've got to get myself cleaned up first."

"I'll wait around and watch TV while you get ready. Do you have any pot left?"

"Yeah, a little. Turn on the fan. My mom doesn't know about that part yet."

When Stephanie got home at seven o'clock that night, she noticed a strange car in the driveway. She went in the side door and headed upstairs to her room.

Her father intercepted her in the hall. "Where have you been?"

"Just over to Jessica's."

"You missed supper."

"I'm not hungry."

"You're to be here for supper whether you're hungry or not. Our home teachers are here. You'd better come in and join us."

"Ah, there's the star of the roadshow," Brother Elliot said as she entered the living room. He and his computer-wizard thirteen-year-old son, Ned, came once a month.

Stephanie sat down.

"Well, Brother Bradshaw, how are things going with your family?"

"We seem to be getting along okay."

"Everyone healthy?"

"Yes."

"How's school going for everybody?"

"Kim got straight A's on her last report card," her father said.

"Good job, Kim."

"Thanks."

"What about you, Stephanie?"

There was an uncomfortable pause.

"Stephanie had a little bad luck last time," her mother said.

"What happened?"

"I didn't get along with some of my teachers, so I got three C's and two B's."

"Those were the first C's she's had," her mother said.

"And we hope the only ones she'll ever get," her father added.

"Gosh, that's as good as I ever got, so don't feel bad. Well, I suppose we ought to get on with the lesson. Ned's going to give it this month. Ned, you all ready?"

Ned read from the *Ensign* magazine, and then they had a prayer. As soon as the home teachers left, Stephanie started for her room.

"Stephanie," her mother said, "what good does it do for me to prepare a meal if you're never here to eat it?"

"I wasn't hungry."

"You need to eat more than you do. You're not looking well lately."

"I'm okay."

28

"Don't make plans for tonight," her father said.

"Why not?"

"Tomorrow we're all going to the Belle Fourche Ward. I don't want you sleeping through church again like you did last week."

"I won't."

"You were out too late last Saturday night."

"I should be able to stay out as late as I want. Jessica can."

"You're not Jessica."

"How about if I come home at one o'clock? That'll give me plenty of sleep."

"You and I could go to a movie," Kim said in an attempt to get Stephanie away from another night of drinking.

"No thanks."

"Tomorrow is the Sabbath day," her father said. "The Sabbath begins at midnight, so that's when you should be in."

"All right, I'll be home at midnight."

"Be sure and wake us up when you come in," he added.

"I will."

It was a great party. Stephanie and Jessica met a bunch of guys from the fraternity, and they all went out of their way to make the girls feel welcome.

"I love this," Jessica said when they had a chance to be alone together.

"I know. College guys are more fun."

They sat around and watched movies and danced and ate pizza and talked and drank beer. After a while everyone sort of paired off. The guy Stephanie ended up was good-looking but too smart for his own good. All he wanted to do was talk politics. In a way it was flattering to Stephanie that he wanted to know her opinions, but it didn't seem she was having as much fun as Jessica, who was slow dancing with the same guy most of the night. Sometime later Jessica left with the guy she was with. They said they were going out for more pizza, but it took them more than an hour, so Stephanie doubted that was all they were doing.

When Jessica returned, she asked Stephanie what time she had to be home.

"I don't know. What time is it?"

"One o'clock."

"Oh. Well, maybe in half an hour."

It was quarter to two when Stephanie finally tiptoed up the stairs to her room. She didn't wake up her parents.

The next thing she remembered was Kim coming into her room. "It's six thirty. We're going with Dad on his high council visit. We need to leave in an hour."

"Pick out an outfit for me to wear. I'll go take a shower to see if I can wake up."

"Why do you take such long showers?"

"I like to be clean."

At the breakfast table, her mother said, "You didn't wake us up when you came in last night."

"No, sorry. I forgot."

"What time was it?"

"Twelve thirty."

"I thought I asked you to be home at midnight," her father said.

"Sorry. We didn't know it was so late."

"What did you do?"

"We just watched movies."

"Where?"

"At one of Jessica's friends."

"Were there parents with you in the home?" her mother asked.

"Yeah, sure."

"What was the rating of the movie you watched?" her father asked.

"PG."

"I just want to make sure you're not watching R-rated movies."

"No. Like if they start showing an R-rated movie, I always go into the kitchen and talk to the parents for a while because I know how you feel about me watching movies like that."

Her parents relaxed. She glanced over at Kim, who was the only one in the family who knew the truth. Kim left the table.

Stephanie felt like she was on display when they walked into the ward in Belle Fourche. There were so few members in the ward that visitors were easily noticed. To top it off, when her father was giving his talk in sacrament meeting, he introduced his family and had them all stand up.

During Sunday School class Stephanie went out to the car and slept. She would have stayed there while Young Women met too, but her mother came out to the car and found her.

"What are you doing out here?"

She was going to say she didn't feel well, but she was afraid her mother would decide not to leave town the next day. "I don't know anybody in there. Besides, how come I have to be dragged along whenever Dad has to go visit another ward?"

"We like to have you with us," her mother said. "You'd better go in now."

Because it was such a small ward, the Mia Maids and the Laurels met together. Stephanie tried to ignore the lesson, but the teacher, assuming the daughter of a high councilor had to be nearly perfect, kept trying to involve her. "Stephanie, what do you do to keep in tune with the Spirit?"

Stephanie was aware that Kim was sitting beside her.

"I pray and read the scriptures and try to do good to other people." She said it in a monotone, as if she were reading it.

"That's good. What do the rest of you do?" No answer. She turned to Kim. "What do you do to stay strong?"

"I do the same as Stephanie."

"Well, that's good. I'm happy to hear that. This is such a tough time for you girls to grow up in. When I was your age, we didn't have half the temptations you have. There's so much evil in the world today. There's alcohol and drugs and such a great emphasis on sex in the movies and on TV. I'm curious about something — maybe you girls can help me. Are there drugs in the schools around here?"

"You can get anything you want in my school," a girl from Belle Fourche said.

The teacher looked at Stephanie. "What about the schools in Rapid City? Are there drugs there?"

"Well, they say there are, but of course I wouldn't know for sure."

The teacher continued. "I just hope you girls will live the Word of Wisdom. The Lord gave it as a warning to us because he loves us and he knew what it would be like for you girls growing up. I read about a girl in today's paper who started using drugs and in one week it killed her. Her heart just gave out on her. If you know of anyone using drugs, I think you should report them to the authorities so they can get help. Kim, do you know anyone in your school who uses drugs?"

"Yes. A girl I know uses drugs and alcohol a lot."

"Have you tried to get her to stop?"

"Yes, but it doesn't seem to do any good."

"Do her parents know what she's doing?"

"No, not yet."

"Would you feel comfortable talking to her parents?"

"Not really."

"Maybe you should see if you can get this girl interested

in the Church. Maybe if she saw she can have fun without drugs, she'd want to quit. I know, maybe you could get her in the roadshow."

"That's a good idea," Kim said.

Stephanie turned to look at her sister. No words were spoken.

The lesson continued.

3

Around four o'clock that afternoon, while Stephanie was sleeping, Kim came to her room. "There's a call for you. It's a guy."

Stephanie leaned over to the bedside stand and picked up the phone. "Hello."

"Hi, this is Craig."

"Let me guess. Rachel's still out of town, right?"

"She'll be back Wednesday. I was wondering if you wanted to do something."

"Like what?"

"I don't know. Drive around."

"All right. Give me fifteen minutes." She paused. "Oh, when you come, could you act like you're kind of interested in my church? That'll make it easier for me to get away."

"No problem."

"Thanks."

"Actually I *am* a little interested. I read a few things in that book you loaned me. Places you'd highlighted. Why did you pick those places?"

"It was for seminary."

"What's seminary?"

"Just a class I used to go to. I'll see you in a few minutes."

As soon as she was ready, she went downstairs. Her father was over at the church having a planning meeting about Family Week. Her mother was fixing one last casserole before she left on their trip.

"I'm going out for a while," Stephanie said.

"Who with?"

"A guy I met Friday night."

"Does he go to your school?"

"No. He graduated last year from Central."

"You know I don't approve of you going out with boys that much older than you."

"Mom, we're just going for a ride. It's no big deal."

"You have to be careful these days. Not every boy has the same standards as you do."

"This is the guy I told you about, the one who's interested in the Church."

"Really? I'd like to meet him."

"Okay."

"One thing though, we've got to have you back here at seven thirty. We're all going out to the airport to meet your grandmother when she comes in. We need you here on time. It's very important we all be there."

"No problem. I'll be here at seven thirty."

When Craig showed up, he had her triple combination. Stephanie introduced him to her mother.

"Stephanie tells me you're interested in the Church," her mother said.

"Yes, I am. Maybe you can help me. I had trouble finding the part Stephanie and I talked about last night, the part that says not to smoke or drink."

"That's section 89 in the Doctrine and Covenants. Stephanie, show him where it is."

Stephanie found the section and put a scrap of paper in to locate it. "Well, we'd better be going now," she said.

As they hurried out to the car, she started laughing. "Bringing the book in with you was a nice touch."

35

"It wasn't totally a lie," he said. "What do you want to do?"

"Go someplace and drink."

"I was thinking of taking you over to meet my parents. We've got a refrigerator that's always pretty well stocked with Bud Light. That's what my dad drinks."

"One beer is not going to do it for me, and I don't want your parents watching me and wondering if I'm ever going to stop."

"Why won't one be enough for you?"

"It never is."

He stopped at a convenience store and bought a six pack, and they took off again. She told him she knew a place near Spearfish where they could go and not be hassled by anyone.

A while later they parked the car and toted the beer up a trail to a waterfall. In the summers people came to swim in the deep hole below the waterfall and to dive off the cliffs of the canyon above the waterfall.

"Have you ever been here before?" she asked.

"No."

"It's called Devil's Bathtub."

They took off their shoes and put their feet in the ice-cold water for a few second, then opened up a couple of beers.

"No after-shave today," he said.

"Great. I've been thinking about that."

"What?"

"Rachel's gone for a few days. Bucky calls you up and asks if you want to go to a keg party. You say yes and then douse yourself with after-shave. Why? Because you're thinking you might meet a girl and you want to make a good impression? But why, when you're practically engaged to Rachel? I think maybe you're not as committed to her as she is to you. What do you say to that?"

"Rachel's the only girl I've ever dated. Sometimes I get

to thinking about that. If we get married next year like we've been talking about, then I'll never know if I married her because it was true love or just because it was easier to stay with her." He paused. "Maybe my parents are right. Maybe I should break up with her and go out with other girls."

"Do it," she said, flashing him a big smile.

After a couple of beers she felt relaxed and happy. She reached down and splashed a little water on him.

"Careful," he warned. "It's too cold for us to get wet."

"I'm not cold, not at all. Are you cold? Good grief, Craig, you're such a wimp." She splashed him again.

"Don't mess with the tiger unless you want to get eaten."

"Oh, wow, what a macho man. Gosh, like I'm really scared." She splashed him in the face.

"That's it, you're history."

After that it was a circus of splashing and shouting and laughing. It ended up with both of them in the pool. By the time they got out, they were freezing.

They ran to the car. He pulled a blanket out of the trunk and gave it to her. She wrapped it around herself. "I can't go home like this," she said.

"Let's go to my place, and my mom can give you something to wear while we put your clothes in the dryer."

"I'm not going to make a great first impression on your parents, am I."

"Don't worry, they'll like you because you're so much fun to be with." He paused. "Rachel isn't half as much fun as you are."

"Hey, nobody is."

When they got to his house, he opened the back door and yelled, "Mom, I've got a girl here who wants to take off her clothes!"

His mother called out from the basement. "Better here

than some other place. Tell her to hold on. I'll be right up."

Craig's father came out into the kitchen. He was barrel-chested and had large, meaty hands. He wasn't quite as tall as Craig, but he had the same warm smile. "What's going on here?"

"Dad, this is Stephanie. We went out to a place called Devil's Bathtub and ended up throwing each other in. We're cold now, and we need to change."

"Stephanie, welcome to our zoo. I suppose Craig has warned you about us by now. I just want to say that most of what he's said is true."

Craig's mother came up the stairs. She was, like her husband, bigger than life and full of energy. But the most noticeable thing about her was her voice, which was, because of thirty years of smoking, deep and raspy. She smiled broadly as she entered the room. "Now what's all this talk about taking off clothes?"

"Mom, this is Stephanie. We kind of got wet, and she needs a change of clothes so we can put her things in the dryer."

"Did mean old Craig get you wet?"

Stephanie grinned. "Yes, that's what happened. I was just sitting there, minding my own business, and he came along and pushed me in."

"What a liar! She started it."

His mother laughed. "Oh, I'll never believe that. Us girls have to stick together, you know." She looked at Stephanie. "I'm not saying I have anything that'll fit you. I haven't looked that good for twenty years, but if you don't mind wearing something a little on the large side, I think I can fix you up."

"I'd be glad for anything just to get out of these wet things."

"Well, okay, come with me and we'll see what we can find."

Craig's parents' bedroom was small compared to even her own, and it was cluttered with framed pictures of the family tacked up on the walls. On a dresser were four bowling trophies, with a fishing hat jauntily perched on one of them. Two bowling balls were on the floor in the closet.

"Excuse the clutter. We're going to get things cleaned up one of these days."

"It's fine."

"Craig's done nothing but talk about you since Friday night. He told us about you two getting stranded in the woods and how you walked out to the highway."

Stephanie was surprised. "He told you that?"

"Oh, sure. That's one thing we've got going with him. He's honest with us. Of course, we don't always approve of everything he does, but the way I figure it, it's better for us to know what's going on. Now let's see what we got here. Last year I got all fired up to lose weight and bought an exercise outfit. See how you like this." She brought it out of the closet. "There. What do you think?"

"It'll be great."

"It's only been used three times," she said. "Of course you can probably tell that, right?"

"You look okay."

"Well, whatever, this is me, like it or not. I'll go get you a towel in case you need it. Oh, the bathroom is just next door. I'll set out the hair dryer for you in there. Anything else you can think of?"

"No. Thank you very much, Mrs. Miller."

"Just call me Peg and my husband is Al. We'd both fall off our chairs if anyone called us anything else."

"I'm sorry to put you to so much trouble . . . Peg."

"Oh, you're no trouble. Besides, I'm glad to meet the second girl who's managed to impress my son. We'd like him to get to know other girls and not just spend all his time with Rachel. He's never gone with anyone except her.

We figure he needs to find out what other girls are like before he settles down. But of course he's like most kids, never listens to us. I mean, what do we know? We're only his parents, right?" She laughed. "Actually it's not that bad. The truth is, Craig's never given us any trouble. We've been real lucky."

"Do you have any other children?"

"No. I lost one in childbirth after him, and then I had some other problems and had to have an operation, and that ended the chance of ever having any more. So we've just got Craig. But enough of this. I'll get out of here so you can get out of those wet things."

After Stephanie changed, she stayed in the room and looked at pictures of the family. She saw Craig as a four-year-old sitting on a pony, held there by his father. It would have been a perfect picture except Craig was crying. She couldn't wait to tease him about it.

The bed was unmade. That in itself was so different from her own mother, who always tried to get all her family to make their beds in the morning. Kim did it obediently, but Stephanie refused, until finally her mother couldn't stand it anymore and started making it for her every morning anyway. Appearances must be kept up, she had heard her mother say time after time.

I'm doing my part to keep up appearances, she thought. *Mother would be so proud of me.*

She picked up her wet things and walked out into the hall. Craig's room was at the end of the hall, and she wanted to go down there and see what it was like. She could see from where she stood that his bed wasn't made either. There was a bulletin board just to the left of the bed with pictures on it. She wanted to go look at them because she wanted to know what Rachel looked like. She hoped she was plain and ordinary. But she didn't go in his room because she was afraid someone would find her there.

She went in the bathroom. There was an ash tray on the counter and several magazines on the clothes hamper. She dried her hair and then borrowed a brush and tried to make it look halfway decent. She could hear occasional comments from Craig and his father in the living room as they watched a baseball game together. They didn't agree on which team would win.

She opened a medicine cabinet and saw a bottle of English Leather after-shave. She opened the top and smelled. It was what Craig had been wearing Friday night. She considered taking it home and putting a little on her pillow at night so she'd dream about him. She would have, but then she thought that maybe it really belonged to Craig's father and that Craig had only borrowed some of it on Friday. At least now she knew the brand name. Maybe she'd buy some on Monday.

Finally she was ready. She went into the kitchen. "I'm done," she said to Peg.

"Here, let me take your wet things and put them in the dryer. You go in with Craig and Al. I'll be back in a minute."

The living room was filled with ranch-style furniture, boxy and comfortable but not fancy. A two-foot-high bowling trophy was on a bookshelf.

"Stephanie," Al said, "you're a reasonable person. Who do you think is going to take the NBA title this year, Boston or L.A.?"

"I don't follow basketball that much."

"I'll help you," Craig said. "Boston's got Bird but he's getting old. So you can forget Boston."

His father interrupted. "Old? I'll show you old. Kareem Abdul-Jabbar is old." He turned to Stephanie to explain. "He's with the Lakers. The Lakers are history."

Stephanie decided Craig was for L.A. but his father liked Boston, so she said, "I think Boston will probably win this year."

"Smart girl!" Al exclaimed.

"Boo!" Craig hooted.

"Don't mind him," Al said. "The boy has no judgment when it comes to sports."

"Oh yeah? Which of us has the most awards from high school football?"

"Anybody can get kiddy awards."

"They weren't kiddy awards."

" 'To the football player with the highest grades.' That's a kiddy award. At least my honors were for playing football."

"There was absolutely no competition when you played football. I mean—after all, the game had just been invented."

"That's all you know."

Peg came in the room. "Hey, you two better behave, 'cause we've got company here. We've got some steaks in the fridge. If I can get some help out of the sports nuts here, we can feed Stephanie some supper."

"There's only one more out left in the game," Craig said.

"I'll help," Stephanie said.

"No, you stay here and try and keep these two apes from killing each other."

The game ended with Craig and his father arguing. "The umpires were on the take," Al said.

"That was a legitimate call," Craig said.

"Maybe you ought to read the rule book once in your life."

Peg called out from the kitchen. "Hey, you two, I need some help in here!"

The three of them hurried in. It was a small kitchen with an oak table that Stephanie later learned Al had built.

"What do you want us to do?" Al asked.

"I need someone to cook the steaks, someone to fix a salad, and someone to set the table."

42

Stephanie ended up fixing the salad, while Craig and Al went out to fire up the grill.

"Those two," Peg said. "Sometimes I feel like the mother of two boys, not just one."

"It's fun to be around your family." Stephanie paused. "My family is mostly serious all the time."

"Why?"

"Because they're trying to be perfect."

"Nobody's perfect."

"I know, but they still keep trying."

"Craig says your parents are going away this week."

"Yes."

Peg smiled. "So you have plans to party, right?"

"Did he tell you that?"

"He didn't have to. I was young once myself."

"Yeah, I have plans."

"What are you planning on doing?"

Stephanie didn't want to say what her plans really were. "Oh, you know, just the usual. I'll skip school and go out to the mall and go shopping. You know, things like that."

"Just don't get involved in drugs, okay? Drugs can kill you."

Stephanie wondered what Craig had told his mother. She thought about telling Peg she was wrong, that drugs and alcohol had given her the greatest happiness she'd ever known in her life, but she knew adults didn't want to hear that.

"And drugs can cause birth defects," Peg said. "I know that doesn't matter to you now, but you're not that far away from it, you know. Three or four or five years from now. Just be careful, okay?"

She didn't pay much attention to the advice, but the way Peg gave it, like she really cared, did have an impact on her.

A few minutes later they sat down to eat.

"Anyone want a beer?" Al called out.

"I'm having water," Peg said.

"Stephanie?"

She looked at Craig. She wasn't sure what to do—it was the first time an adult had ever offered her a beer.

"I'll have one," Craig said to help her decide.

"I guess I will too," Stephanie said.

"Craig says you're a Mormon," Al said a few minutes later.

She glanced at the can of beer in front of her plate. "Well, yeah, sort of. Not a very good one though."

"Hey, you don't have to apologize to us. We think you're fine just the way you are. Around here we take people as they come, warts and all."

"I think you should think about becoming a Catholic," Craig said to her. "Then you could drink and nobody'd say a thing about it."

"That might be better than the way it is now." She paused. "My parents don't know I drink yet."

"Tell 'em," Peg said.

"I'm not sure they could handle it."

"Parents usually can handle whatever they need to. It's better for parents to know what's happening, no matter how bad it is, than for their kids to keep everything hidden."

"I suppose."

"That's one thing about Craig. He tells us what's going on."

"I wish it was that way between my parents and me, but it isn't."

"Maybe you need to be the one to make the first move," Peg said.

"You're probably right."

They ate, and then she and Craig did dishes and then watched TV with his parents. After the first half hour show her clothes were dry, so she went in the bathroom and

44

changed. Before she left the bathroom she dabbed some of the after-shave on her wrist.

"You look a lot better in that," Craig said with a big smile. "I mean, my mom's clothes were *so* huge for you . . . Like a five-man tent . . . "

"Watch it, buster, or you'll get shoe leather in your sandwich tomorrow," Peg said.

"You want another beer?" Craig asked.

She hesitated.

"I'm going to have one," he said.

"Well, okay, I guess one more won't hurt."

"You two know where they're kept, don't you?" Peg said. "Help yourself."

They went in the kitchen. Craig leaned close to her. "What's that smell?" He sniffed. "It's my after-shave, isn't it?"

She knew her face was turning a bright red. "Yes."

"Why'd you put on my after-shave?"

"This is really embarrassing."

"C'mon, tell me."

She hesitated. "I wanted it so I'd dream about you tonight."

For him that was the ultimate compliment. "Yeah? I thought you didn't like it."

"I've changed my mind. Let's go back."

The Sunday night movie began with a scene of an airplane landing. That's when Stephanie remembered. "Oh no!"

"What's wrong?"

"I was supposed to go out with my parents to pick up my grandmother, and I forgot all about it. My mother is going to kill me. I'd better go home before I get in any worse trouble."

A few minutes later when they got to her place, Craig said, "I'll go in with you."

"What for?"

45

"To apologize. It was my fault for keeping you out so long."

"You don't have to do that."

"No, but I'm going to do it anyway."

When they walked into the living room, Stephanie's grandmother was listening to Kim play the piano. "Gramma, how are you? I'm so sorry I missed you at the airport."

"Stephanie, darling! Don't worry about that. Come here and let me give you a hug."

She was soon enveloped by her grandmother's soft hug. She smelled, as always, like lilacs in bloom.

"Who's your friend?" Gramma asked.

"This is Craig Miller."

"Craig, it's nice to meet you."

"I was at Craig's house watching TV with his parents. I forgot all about going to meet you at the airport."

Kim got up from the piano.

"Kim, don't go. You haven't finished your piece yet," her grandmother said. "Craig, this is Kim, Stephanie's sister."

"Hi, Kim."

"Hello." Kim turned to her grandmother. "I can do this for you later."

"No, do it now. This way we'll have two more in your audience."

Kim played the rest of the piece.

Stephanie noticed Craig watching Kim play the rest of the piece. She tried to look at her the way she thought he would. Kim looked a little like Alice in Wonderland with her blond hair and serious blue eyes. She played the piano the way she lived her life, with control and precision but no spontaneity.

"Well, that was wonderful," Gramma said. "I didn't hear one mistake."

"Thank you," Kim said.

"It really was good," Craig said. He turned to Stephanie. "You didn't tell me your sister was better looking than you."

"I didn't think you'd be interested."

Kim was embarrassed and left. Stephanie's mother came in the room. "Where on earth have you been?"

Craig broke in. "Mrs. Bradshaw, this is all my fault. We were up at Devil's Bathtub and I threw her in, so we had to come back and dry off."

"Where did you go to dry off?"

"We went to my place."

"Your apartment?"

"No. I live at home."

"Were your parents home?"

"Yes."

Her mother turned to Stephanie. "When I ask you to be somewhere, I expect you to be there, or if you can't make it, I expect at least a phone call informing me of that fact. We waited ten extra minutes for you, which made us late at the airport, which meant that my mother had to get off the plane and not be met by anyone. What was she supposed to think? That we'd forgotten all about her? That we didn't care that much about her to even make an effort to be there on time? You are always pushing me to the limit, and I want it to stop. Do you understand me?"

"I said I was sorry," Stephanie said, her anger beginning to show.

"What were you doing at Devil's Bathtub anyway?"

"Craig said he'd never been there before. I just wanted to show him what it's like."

"I need to speak to you alone in my room."

Craig took the hint. "I'd better go. I'll call you tomorrow."

As soon as he left, her mother asked to speak to her privately. They went to Stephanie's room and closed the door. "I don't see how I can leave town tomorrow now,"

47

her mother said. "What's going on between you and Craig?"

"Nothing. We're just friends. Besides, he's already going with someone."

"I don't like the idea of you going out with someone who isn't a member of the Church."

"Look, if you're worried, I'll promise not to see him until you get back, if that'll make you feel any better."

"Can I trust you?"

"Mom, you know you can. Go with Daddy to California. You know you've both been looking forward to it."

"All right, if you promise to behave."

"I will. You go and have fun. Everything'll be fine here."

That night Craig sat down at his desk and opened the triple combination Stephanie had loaned him. He turned to the place she'd marked. It was verse six that first caught his attention. "Thus saith the Lord unto you: In consequence of evils and designs which do and will exist in the hearts of conspiring men in the last days, I have warned you, and forewarn you, by giving unto you this word of wisdom by revelation — That inasmuch as any man drink wine or strong drink among you, behold it is not good."

He glanced through other sections in the book that Stephanie had marked in seminary. He found in section one the following underlined in red: "What I the Lord have spoken, I have spoken, and I excuse not myself; and though the heavens and the earth pass away, my word shall not pass away, but shall all be fulfilled, whether by mine own voice or by the voice of my servants, it is the same."

The boldness of the words struck him. The words "I the Lord saith unto you . . . " rang in his mind.

4

On Monday morning Stephanie drove her parents out to the airport. She made sure the plane took off before she went back to her car. On the way home she put in one of the tapes her parents hated and played it as loud as it would go. "It's time to party!" she called out to a couple of guys at a stoplight. They followed her for a while, until she pulled into the high school parking lot.

She went to her first-period class because it was art and she liked the teacher. During second period she worked in the office. It was volunteer service she had begun a year earlier.

This week she had a special reason for wanting to work in the office. The phone rang. She quickly picked it up. "Stevens High School."

"Hello. This is Mrs. Phillips. My daughter Jessica is sick today, so I'd like to have her excused." The voice on the other end was, of course, Jessica's.

Stephanie had to be careful in case someone was listening in. "Yes, of course, Mrs. Phillips, we can do that. Thank you for calling. Goodbye." She hung up and wrote out an excuse for Jessica.

Four other friends called in for excuses while she was

working. Since she could not excuse herself, the next hour she would phone in and have a friend excuse her.

There was one more service she did for her friends while working in the office. When a student missed three classes in a row, the teacher sent a referral form to the vice-principal, who would then notify the parents. Each day Stephanie went through the stack of referral forms and pulled out the ones for herself and her friends. After that she was free to skip school for the rest of the day.

At ten o'clock Stephanie arrived at Jessica's place. She changed into a tattered Ratt T-shirt and jeans. When it was time to go home, she would change back to what she'd worn to school that morning.

Her friends drifted in and out most of the day. Stephanie bankrolled everything. At noon she drove to the bank-teller machine for some money, and a friend with an ID went out for more beer. At four o'clock Jessica kicked everyone out of the house so she could get rid of any signs of their having been there. One of the partygoers took all the empties and drove to a park and tossed them on the lawn.

Once Stephanie got home, she went straight to her room and closed the door and lay down on the bed. She felt a little sick.

Kim came in a while later. "Gramma says that supper is ready."

"I'm not hungry."

"You still better come down and eat."

"Why?"

"Because if you don't, she'll be worried about you." Stephanie sat on the edge of the bed. "How do I look?"

"Awful. Did you party today?"

"Yeah."

"Don't do it anymore this week, okay?"

"It's no big deal."

"I hate what you're doing to yourself."

50

"I can handle it."

"Why do you hang around the druggies all the time?"

"They're my friends."

"Look, if you want to skip classes tomorrow, let me go with you. We'll go to Sheridan Lake and take a picnic lunch. We'll have fun, just the two of us. You don't need those people, Stephanie. Or we could go bowling or go for a hike or just about anything you want to do. Anything. Just stay away from Jessica and all her friends."

Stephanie paused. "They're my friends too."

"I don't mean anything to you, do I."

"No, that's not true. You're important to me. I just need to be with my friends tomorrow, that's all."

"Were you with Craig today?"

"No. He works for his dad during the day. Besides, he's not that much of a party animal."

"What are you going to do when report cards come out?"

"I'll worry about that when it happens."

"You're going to flunk everything, aren't you."

She shrugged her shoulders. "Grades aren't everything."

"All right then, don't pay any attention to what I say." Kim hurried out of the room.

On Tuesday evening Stephanie was home, playing the part of the dutiful child and at the same time trying to recover from an all-day party. At eight o'clock she went to bed.

A little after nine o'clock the doorbell rang. Kim was watching TV. She answered the door. It was Craig. "Is Stephanie here?"

"She's upstairs. Come in. I'll go get her."

Craig waited in the living room.

A few minutes later Kim came down. "She says she's

not feeling very good and can you come back tomorrow night?"

"Okay." He noticed Kim's expression. "Are you all right?"

"Not really."

"Anything I can do?"

"Can I talk to you?"

"Sure."

"Is it okay if we talk in your car? I don't want my grandmother to hear."

They went out and sat in his car in the driveway. Kim began. "The way Stephanie's going, I think she's going to end up killing herself."

"Did she skip school again today?"

"Yes. I keep trying to make her stop, but she never listens to me."

"Maybe it's time to tell your parents what's happening."

"I promised Stephanie I wouldn't say anything. Besides, Stephanie says that as soon as Mom and Dad get back, she's going to quit."

"Do you think she will?"

"I don't know. She has to do something or else she's going to flunk out. She hardly ever goes to any of her classes anymore, and grades are coming out soon. Will you talk to her? Maybe she'll listen to you."

"All right."

"She'll be at Jessica's house all day tomorrow."

"I might be able to drop by during my lunch hour."

She gave him Jessica's address.

Just then the front door opened and Kim's grandmother, in robe and slippers, came outside and walked over to the car. "Kim, what are you doing out here?"

Kim and Craig both got out. "We were just talking," Kim said.

Gramma turned to Craig. "I think it's far too late for Kim to be out on a school night."

"We were just talking," Kim said.

"What's so important that it can't wait until tomorrow?"

"We were talking about Stephanie," Craig answered.

"Craig wanted to know if Stephanie liked him or not," Kim added quickly.

"Why doesn't Craig ask Stephanie herself that question?" She turned to Craig. "I really don't think it's a good idea for you to be here while the girls' parents are away. Kim, please go into the house and get ready for bed."

"Goodbye, Craig. Thanks for talking to me."

Late that night Emily called home to see how things were going. She heard the report about Craig and Kim being in the car together. She was confused. "You don't mean Kim, do you?"

"Yes, that's who I mean. They said they were talking about Stephanie. I told him it would be better if he were to stay away this week. You can sort it out after you get back."

That night Emily couldn't sleep, worrying about what was going on back home. When she talked to David about it, he reminded her that they'd be going home in only two more days. And besides, what Kim said—that she and Craig were only talking about Stephanie—was probably true.

That night Kim lay in bed and thought what it would be like if Craig really was interested in her. *I'd be so good for him,* she thought just before falling asleep.

During his lunch hour on Wednesday, Craig drove over to Jessica's house. There were five cars in the driveway. He knocked, and Jessica came to the door.

"Is Stephanie here?"

"Yeah, just a minute."

53

Stephanie came to the door. She was wearing Jessica's Motley Crue T-shirt and had a red sweat band around her forehead. "Why, if it isn't my old buddy Craig. Hey, did you come to party?" She slurred the words together.

"No. Can I talk to you?"

"Sure you can. Come on in and have a beer."

"No, thanks. Can we talk in my car?"

They walked to his car. "So," she teased, "I hear you're hustling my little sister."

"You know that's not true."

"That's not what Gramma says. All through breakfast we heard about what happened last night. It was *so* funny. Gramma warned us we were roses and that we needed to be careful because guys like you were out to pick us before we had truly blossomed. I'm serious, those were her exact words. 'Truly blossomed.' It was *so* hilarious. I could hardly keep a straight face."

"I went over there to see you but you were asleep. Kim said she wanted to talk to me. We sat in my car and talked until your grandmother came out and made Kim go in."

"What did my little sister want to talk to you about?"

"She's worried about you."

"What for? I've got everything under control."

"Kim says you're flunking school."

"No problem, I can handle it. Is that why you dragged me out here, to talk about education in these troubled times? Or do you just want to fool around?" She slid next to him and ran her finger lightly across his lips. "You really get to me, you know that? I mean, in a major way."

He brushed her hand away. "C'mon, Stephanie, settle down."

"Settle down? You sound just like a teacher I used to have in the third grade. Mrs. Aldrich was her name. 'You children settle down or you'll all have to stay after class.' You sound just like her. I'm serious. It's like you're the ghost of Mrs. Aldrich." She made an eerie ghostlike sound and then burst out laughing.

"I've started reading the Book of Mormon."

"You want some advice, Craig? Don't become a Mormon. Everyone is always on you to do better. Well, I don't want to do better. I don't want to do anything. I just want to be left alone."

"If you know God doesn't want you to live the way you're living, why do you do it?"

"There's lots of things God doesn't want people to do, but they do them anyway. God doesn't want people to murder, but then there's a war, and people put on a uniform and they go out and kill each other."

"That's different."

"That's the way it is with my drinking—it's different."

"I can't understand you."

"Who asked you to?"

"You've got to quit doing this to yourself."

"It's just this week while my mom and dad are gone. Next week I'll be the perfect little angel I've always been. Mommy and Daddy are so proud of their perfect little angel."

"I've got to go now."

"Aw, come on and have a beer before you go."

"No."

"One beer isn't going to hurt you. I'm buying for everybody."

"No." He got out and went around the car and opened her door. She didn't budge. "Get out, Stephanie. I've got to go to work."

"Carry me into the house."

"You can walk."

"Haven't you ever wanted to carry a girl across the threshold?"

"C'mon, I really need to go now."

"Carry me back to the house or I'll stay in here forever."

There was no other way to get rid of her. He reached in and picked her up and started for the house.

"Why aren't you any fun anymore? Nobody's any fun anymore. Not even my old buddy Jessica. She says there's too many people here today. Just because I told everyone at school we were going to party and I was paying for everything." She touched his biceps. "You're really strong, aren't you? You have great arm muscles. You must work out all the time. I love your face, though, best of all. You have the most wonderful face. I've got an idea. Why don't you just leave your face here with me when you go to work." She giggled. "That was a joke — why aren't you laughing? Oh, homeboy, don't you know how much I love you? Stay here with me for the afternoon, or if you want, we'll take a drive up in the hills. Look, if you're worried about me, bring Rachel along. There's plenty enough beer for her too."

"You're drunk, Stephanie."

"That's not the half of what I am, but who cares? I dream about you at night. And when I first wake up in the morning I think about us."

They got to the door and he set her down.

"Aren't you going to carry me across the threshold?" she said. "That's what guys are supposed to want to do. Why don't you want to? Am I so awful to you? Well, there's plenty of guys who'd like to carry me across the threshold, but I never let 'em because they're all such clowns. And then you come along. We have one perfect time together and then everything turns bad. Why are you looking at me that way? Do you think I'm so horrible? If you don't like me now, think how it'll be when I've lost all my hair. Oh, didn't you know I'm going bald? My hair just falls out in big lumps. I'm like a cocker spaniel that's shedding. I used to have a cocker spaniel. His name was Prince. He was a wonderful dog, but my parents took him away be- cause he messed up their perfect house. You see, everything has to be perfect in their house. And if it's not, they get rid of it. Like they're going to get rid of me someday, but I don't care because I'm leaving anyway. I want to be in the movies or even TV. I'm not particular. Don't laugh. It could happen. There's such a demand for bald actresses these days. Like I could be on 'Star Trek,' you know. A female creature from some other solar system. That's the way I feel anyway. Don't go. Come in and meet some of my friends. Come and meet Jessica. I know she's inside drooling over you anyway. She's *so* shallow, not like me at all, right?"

"Stephanie."

"What?"

He stared at her. "I really feel sorry for you." He turned and walked away.

She yelled out after him. "Hey, don't feel sorry for me, 'cause at least I'm living life. Go ahead and be a Mormon and start hanging around with Kim. You two would be perfect together. You could both go around quietly disapproving of everything I do. Listen to me. I don't care what happens here because I'm going to California and get rich and famous. You'll see. I don't need you. I don't need anybody."

He drove away.

Stephanie swore and went inside and snorted some crank.

Later that day Stephanie used her mother's bank card to withdraw one hundred and fifty dollars. By the time the day was over, she had spent it all on drugs and beer for herself and her friends.

That night she showed up for the roadshow practice in bad shape. On stage she kept slurring words together and forgetting the simplest of directions. And then after the third time of being corrected on a five-word line, she started laughing and couldn't stop. "I'm sorry . . . it's just that this whole thing is so funny . . . I'm sorry. I'll get it . . . this time . . . this is so funny . . . No, wait . . . I'll do it this time . . . I'll get it. This is so crazy . . . I know I can do this . . . I'm going to be a movie star some-day . . . so this is good practice for me . . . "

She noticed the way people were looking at her. Kim came up on stage. "Stop it! You're making a fool of yourself."

"You're just jealous. You've always been jealous of me because I live life in the fast lane."

"Do it the way you're supposed to!" Kim shouted. She stormed out of the cultural hall.

After Stephanie finished her part, she went looking for Kim. She found her in the car. She got in. "You calmed down yet?"

"Everyone at church knows about you now. Mom's going to find out."

"I don't care. If anybody gives me any grief about the way I live my life, I'll pack up and leave. From now on I'm not taking nothin' from nobody. Let's get out of here."

5

On Thursday morning, when Stephanie reported for work in the school office, she was met by the secretary. "You can't work here anymore."

"What are you talking about?"

"Teachers are sending in referrals about you but they're not making it to Mr. Simmons. Yesterday we found out you've been pulling them out. We found some in the wastebasket yesterday after you left. Not only for you but for all your friends too."

"I don't know what you're talking about."

"This entire week you've been skipping school after you leave here, haven't you?"

"I've had the flu."

"Don't give me that. I want a reasonable explanation of what's been going on."

"I don't have a reasonable explanation."

"Mr. Simmons wants to talk to your mother."

"My parents are out of town. I'm serious."

"I don't believe anything you say anymore." The secretary phoned Stephanie's grandmother. ". . . Our vice-principal, Mr. Simmons, would like to talk to Stephanie's parents when they come home. When will that be? . . . I see. Will you give them the message when they get in tonight? Perhaps they could come in tomorrow morning . . . Thank you. Goodbye." She hung up. "You'd better go now. I'm so disappointed in you for betraying the trust we had in you. Get out of here before I get really mad."

Stephanie didn't skip school that day. Instead she went to each class and stayed after to talk to her teachers. She told them she'd been sick and that she really wanted to make up the work she'd missed. Because of her past history of being a good student, most of them believed her.

At noon she and Jessica went over to Jessica's house. They smoked some pot and had a couple of beers and talked about what was going to happen. "If things get too bad," Jessica said, "you can always come and stay here."

"That'd be so great to get away from my family. The only thing I'd miss is the bank card."

"If you need money, you can always become a dealer. They make good money, and, another thing, I hear they get free samples too."

"Sounds good."

All week she had been driving her mother's car because it was new and because there was nobody around to tell her not to. On the way home she stopped at a convenience store for some mouthwash. When she took off again, she wasn't paying attention and ran into a parked car, putting a big dent on the right side of her mother's car. She drove it home and parked it in the garage. Then she piled up some food storage boxes in front of the dent so it couldn't be seen.

Gramma asked her why the school wanted to talk to her parents.

"I think it's about me joining National Honor Society," Stephanie said.

"Well, that's nice."

"Yes, it's quite an honor."

At supper Stephanie said, "You stay here, Gramma,

and relax. Kim and I'll go to the airport to pick up Mom and Dad."

When Stephanie and Kim went to the garage, Stephanie had to move some of the boxes so she could back out.

"What happened to the car?" Kim asked.

"Somebody ran into me."

"What are you going to tell Mom and Dad?"

"Don't worry about it. Just leave everything to me, okay?"

Their parents' plane was on time. After waiting to get their suitcases, they proceeded out to the car. "What's this?" Stephanie's father said, looking at the dent.

"Gosh, I don't know." Stephanie was wide-eyed with surprise. "I guess someone must have run into us while we were parked."

Her father checked to see if the person who'd hit them had left a note.

"Gosh, some people," Stephanie complained. "Why would someone just hit us and then drive away?"

"They probably don't have insurance. It looks to be about a thousand dollars' damage."

"That much?" Stephanie said.

"Well, this is quite the welcome home, isn't it?" her mother said. "What else has gone wrong?"

"Nothing."

"Has Craig been around since Gramma caught him in the car with Kim?"

"Mother, you make it sound like we were doing something wrong," Kim said. "We were just talking. Why doesn't anyone believe me?"

"Because you're like a beautiful young rose about to blossom," Stephanie teased, trying to sound sincere for her mother's sake but knowing Kim would understand she was being sarcastic.

"Craig hasn't been around," Kim said.

61

"Well, at least that's one thing to be glad of," her mother said.

At home there was so much to catch up on that Gramma forgot to report that Mr. Simmons wanted to talk, as Stephanie had led her to believe, about the National Honor Society.

Stephanie took a long shower so she'd be able to relax and get some sleep. She wondered if Mr. Simmons would forget about talking to her parents. Maybe it would all just go away. At least the marijuana made her think so anyway.

The next morning Stephanie was called out of her second class and asked to report to the office. When she got there, she saw through an open door her mother talking to Mr. Simmons.

"Sit down," the secretary said. "They'll be ready for you in a minute."

Stephanie sat and tried to think of the possibilities. She knew that if it got too bad, she could always leave home. Jessica would hide her until she could get to California and get a job and be on her own.

Ten minutes later Mr. Simmons asked her in. He was as old and gray as his suit. He had a habit that when he looked at a person, it was through the bottom part of his bifocals so that it appeared he was looking down on everyone. Today he was the voice of gloom. " . . . flunking in history, flunking in algebra, flunking in chemistry . . . unexcused absences in her classes this week . . . Also we think she's been using her office duties to excuse her friends and hide the absence forms teachers have sent in about her."

Her mother was in total shock. "What on earth is going on here? Where have you been when you should have been in school?"

"I've just been going to the mall with my friends, that's all."

"What did you do all this week?"

"Mom, everybody ditches when their parents leave town."

"Were you with Craig?"

"No."

"Don't lie to me."

"I wasn't with Craig, Mom. I just went to the mall with some friends."

"Why?"

"I like to shop."

"Stephanie, look at me," Mr. Simmons said. "What are you on?"

"What do you mean?"

"Don't play dumb with me. You're using something. What is it? Liquor? Pot? Speed? Cocaine? What is it?"

"I don't know what you're talking about. I'm a Mormon. Mormons don't believe in drinking or smoking."

Stephanie was aware of the way her mother was staring at her. She knew her face was turning red. She ran her fingers through her hair and then stared at the dead hair that had come out.

She denied everything. Mr. Simmons suggested that she go home and try to work things out with her parents and that on Monday she come back serious about school again and prepared to make up the work she'd missed.

It's not so bad, she thought as she walked with her mother to the car. True, her parents would be on her case about schoolwork now, but even so, it could be worse.

They got in the car.

"You're the one who wrecked the car, aren't you," her mother said. It was a statement, not a question.

"No, it's like I said. Someone ran into us at the airport while we went in to get you."

Her mother didn't turn at the road to their home.

"Where are we going?"

"We're going to have a talk."

She drove to the parking lot of Dinosaur Park and stopped.

"What are you on, Stephanie?"

"Nothing."

"Don't give me that. Mr. Simmons was on the right track, wasn't he?"

"No. Why is everyone picking on me all of a sudden?"

Her mother was losing her patience. "Tell me what it is you're doing!"

"Nothing."

"We're not moving until you tell me the truth, even if we have to stay here all night."

Minutes passed by. "Mom, this is ridiculous. There's nothing for me to say."

"Don't lie to me."

"Why is it you believe Mr. Simmons and not me?"

Half an hour passed. Finally Stephanie said, "All right, I have tried beer, but it was just a couple of times."

"What else?"

"That's all. I swear."

"You're lying."

Five minutes later. "All right, I tried pot too, but just one time."

"What else?"

"I might have tried speed once too."

"Is that it?"

"Yes, that's the whole truth. I was kind of worried about telling you, but I'm glad it's out in the open now."

Her mother was satisfied. "I'm glad you told me. We'll do whatever we need to do to help you. It can't happen again, Stephanie. It just can't."

"It won't. I promise."

They drove in silence the rest of the way home. When they got home, Stephanie went straight to her room and stayed there. At six o'clock she saw her father drive up. She waited. Ten minutes later he knocked on her door.

"Come in," she said.

He opened the door. "I need to talk to you."

"Okay."

He pulled up a chair and sat down next to the bed, where she was lying down. He looked visibly shaken. "Your mother has just told me some things about you that were very hard for me to believe. First of all, I want you to know that no matter what's happened, we still love you. And we're going to work with you and do whatever it takes to get you off drugs and alcohol."

"It was just something I tried, Daddy, but now I can see it's no good, so I'm not ever going to use any of it again."

"I'm glad you feel that way."

"I'm sorry I caused you and Mom to worry."

"The important thing is to get you back on track."

"I can stop it all today. No problem. And I'll start getting caught up on my classes too. Everything's going to work out okay, you'll see."

"Good." He sighed. "Is it okay if your mother comes in now?"

"Sure."

He called Emily. When she came in, he said, "Stephanie says she's willing to give it all up."

"Oh, Stephanie, that's so good."

Her father cleared his throat. "I'd like to give you a priesthood blessing to help you not use anything from now on."

"I'd like that, Daddy."

She sat in the chair, and he placed his hands on her head and gave her a blessing. She had never before heard him so emotional, and it made her cry. Her mother cried too. Afterwards they both came to her and put their arms around her and told her how much they loved her. And then they left her in her room.

Half an hour later Kim came in the room. "Mom says for me to tell you supper is ready."

"Tell her I'm not hungry."

"They know everything now, don't they?" Kim asked.

"Yes."

"I knew they'd find out sometime. I didn't tell them anything."

"I know. Thanks, Kim."

Kim left, and a few minutes later her mother came in. "Even if you're not hungry, can't you just come down and be with us?"

She nodded.

It was very quiet at supper.

"I got an A in a test today," Kim said.

"That's very good. You're taking after your sister." It was an awkward moment. "In your classes, I mean . . . I mean, the way Stephanie was . . . before this happened."

Stephanie looked at her grandmother. She could tell nobody had told her what was happening. Stephanie was glad about that. Gramma would be leaving in the morning.

Kim was the only one who ate very much. As soon as she was through, she excused herself and went upstairs.

Stephanie got up. "I think I'll go back to my room now. I've got a lot of studying to catch up on." She paused. "I think maybe I'll take a shower first though."

"Fine. That'll clear your mind."

She suppressed a smile. "Yes, it always does."

She smoked pot in the bathroom before her shower.

Stephanie stayed home all day Saturday. In the morning she sat at the kitchen table and did homework. At noon she took a shower and got high. In the afternoon she talked on the phone with Jessica. Jessica was going over to the fraternity house that night, and she wanted Stephanie to go with her.

"I can't."

"C'mon, you can sneak out after your parents go to bed. We'll pick you up around midnight."

"No, I really can't."

"We'll come by at midnight and wait for you at the corner anyway."

Stephanie watched TV with her mother and Kim until ten, and then her parents went to bed. At eleven thirty, Kim went to bed. At eleven forty-five Stephanie went up to her room. She sat down on her bed and tried to decide what to do. She wanted to go with Jessica to the fraternity party, but she knew that if her parents caught her out late at night without permission, they'd never let her out of their sight again. It didn't make sense to risk everything when she had everything she needed to make her happy right in her own home.

She kept telling herself she wasn't going, but at five minutes to midnight she stood at the window, her jacket in her hand, waiting for a car to appear at the corner.

She waited until one o'clock, but no one came. At one thirty she finally went to bed.

The next day she want to church with her parents. After church she went to her room, and while her mother took a nap, she turned on the shower and smoked some pot. It made the rest of the afternoon bearable.

That night she talked to Jessica on the phone. Jessica said she was sorry she hadn't come by the night before but she'd had a chugalug contest with some guy and passed out and ended up spending the night sprawled out on a couch in the fraternity house.

At nine o'clock Sunday evening her father knocked on her door. "We'd like to have family prayer now."

"Okay, Daddy."

After family prayer her parents hugged her again. And then her father asked to speak to her. "When you go to

67

school tomorrow, there'll be people there who'll want you to continue to use drugs and alcohol, won't there?"

"Yeah, Daddy, I guess there will be."

"What'll you do if someone offers you something?"

"I'll tell 'em I've given it up."

"It might be hard to say that the first couple of times."

She shrugged her shoulders. "Not really."

"I want you to tell me whenever it happens. Even if you use again, I want to know. I want us to be close. This is a conflict between good and evil. Anytime you want a priesthood blessing, just let me know. And tomorrow night, I'll want to know exactly what happened in school. Will you be honest with me?"

"Sure, Daddy, I will. There's no reason for me to lie now because you know everything."

"We can beat this thing."

"If you ask me, it's already beat. It's a good thing we stopped it before it got to be too much of a problem."

"I love you, Stephanie."

"I love you too, Daddy."

"You're my pride and joy."

"I won't let you down. You'll see."

6

David Bradshaw got up each morning at five o'clock. On Monday, after getting dressed, he read the scriptures and then wrote in his journal. That morning he wrote the following:

> Last Friday we learned that Stephanie has been drinking and also that she's tried marijuana and speed once. It was a painful thing for us to find out, but fortunately I think we found out early enough. We had a long talk yesterday and I gave her a priesthood blessing so she would be able to quit.
>
> The one good thing to come out of this is that for the first time in such a long time I feel close to her and she's willing to confide in me. We'll talk every day after school, and she'll tell me the times she was tempted to use drugs or drink, and we'll talk about how she did. I feel that we'll be able to conquer this if we work at it together.
>
> It shows how much the adversary works to deceive the very elect. The age-old conflict between good and evil continues on.
>
> I can't help but wonder why this is happening to us. We have family home evenings, we go to church, we pray as a family. What more could we do?

I'm not sure if President Winder will want to
keep me on as a member of the high council or
not. My family is certainly not setting a very good
example right now.

Stephanie stayed in school all day Monday, except during lunch when she went to Jessica's home and tried cocaine for the first time. It was the most incredible thing she'd ever tried, but very expensive. She decided she would have to find a way to get more.

She got home from school at four o'clock. Her father had quit work early so he'd be there when she got home. He asked to speak to her. They went to his office and sat down.

"What happened today?" he asked.

She tried to make up a story he would believe. "Well, this guy came up and offered me a joint."

"Joint? That's marijuana, isn't it? Or should I call it pot?"

"Either is okay."

"What did you tell him?"

"I told him no, Daddy, just like we talked about."

"Good for you. What did he say to that?"

"He said I'd never be able to quit. I told him I would so. And he goes, 'What makes you so sure?' And I go, 'Because my dad holds the priesthood.' I knew he didn't understand that, but that's what I told him all right."

Her father's eyes moistened. "Your mother and I are proud of you. We know this isn't easy."

"No, but with your help, I'm sure I can beat this thing."

"I'll be here tomorrow for you too, when you come home from school. And if you need to phone me during school, please do. I want to be available for you."

"Thanks a lot."

"There's just one other thing we should maybe talk about. Do you have your billfold with you?"

"Yeah, why?"

"I need to get back your mother's bank card."

She panicked. She needed the bank card for cocaine tomorrow. "What for?"

"Today your mother went to the bank, and they told her all the money you withdrew while we were gone. That was for drugs and alcohol, wasn't it?"

"Not all of it. I had to pay for the school annual."

"How much was the annual?"

"Fifteen dollars."

"Do you know how much you've withdrawn from the bank in the last week?"

"No."

"Over four hundred dollars."

"It can't be that much. The bank must have made a mistake."

"There's no mistake. We had them check it for us. They can tell us the exact times you were there. May I have the card back?"

"I won't do it again, Daddy. Really. I've learned my lesson."

"Even so, I still need you to give me back the card."

"I'll still need money for school expenses."

"You can come to us for money when you need it."

She gave him the card.

Later that night she went to see Kim in her room. "I need to borrow some money."

"All I've got is ten dollars."

"Don't lie to me, Kim. I know you've got more than that. You never spend any of your money."

"It's in the bank."

"I need to pay back somebody I owe money to."

"How much do you owe?"

"A hundred dollars."

"Maybe you ought to go see Daddy about that."

"You know I can't do that. C'mon, you've got to help me out."

"I'm not giving you a hundred dollars."

"Fifty then. Come on, it'll just be for a couple of days."

Kim went to a sock in her gym bag and pulled out a twenty-dollar bill and gave it to Stephanie.

"It's not enough."

"Nothing's ever enough for you, is it?"

Stephanie took the money and returned to her room.

Kim called Craig Tuesday evening after he got home from work. She told him her parents knew about Stephanie's drinking and that she was trying to stop.

"Do you think she's going to quit for good?" he asked.

"I don't know, but at least it's out in the open. It might help if you'd talk to her."

"Is she home now?"

"Yeah. She's in her room."

"Let me talk to her."

A minute later Stephanie picked up the phone in her bedroom. "Hi there, homeboy, how's it going?"

"Okay. How are you doing?"

"Better than the last time you saw me. Look, I'm really sorry about the way I was at Jessica's. I was pretty much out of it."

"Yeah, I know. I understand."

"Did Kim tell you what's been happening around here?"

"Yeah." He paused. "Your parents knowing about it is probably the best thing that could've happened."

"Yeah, sure."

"You want to do anything tonight?" he asked.

"Are you serious? After I made such a fool of myself at Jessica's, I figured I'd never hear from you again. What made you decide to call me again?"

"Actually Kim called me."

"You know what? I think Kim's found true love."

"Very funny. She just wanted me to know about you. Look, do you want to go out tonight?"

"Yeah, let's take Kim with us and go up to where we first met."

"Why do you want to take Kim?"

Stephanie paused. "She needs to get to know you better."

Kim was "it," and Craig and Stephanie were hiding together.

Stephanie snuggled up to him but he didn't respond.

"Feeling a little guilty because you haven't talked to Rachel?" she asked.

"Yes."

Kim called out. "Hey, you guys! I give up! Where are you?"

"We'd better go back," he said.

"No, let her sweat it out."

Craig called out. "We're coming!"

They met at the campsite. "Where'd you two go?" Kim asked.

"Just up that hill."

"It's not fair. I shouldn't have to go searching through the whole forest for you two."

"You're right," Stephanie said. "This time I'll be 'it' and you two can go hide."

Craig and Kim ran to the far end of the campgrounds and sat down at a picnic table.

"Ready or not, here I come!" Stephanie shouted in the distance.

As they waited, Kim broke the silence. "I think getting Stephanie out here is good for her, don't you?"

"I don't know. I hope so."

"I wish she'd never started drinking," Kim said. "I know one thing. I'm never going to start." She paused. "You think you'll ever come to church with us?"

"Maybe. I've got to talk to Rachel first. She and I usually go to our own church."

"You're sort of torn between Rachel and Stephanie, aren't you?"

"Yeah, sort of. Stephanie's so much fun to be with. If she ever gets her life straightened out, she'll be everything I've ever wanted."

"You should keep learning about the Church so if things work out, you and she could be married in the temple someday."

"Have you ever read the Book of Mormon?" he asked.

"Yes."

"What do you think about it?"

"I know it's true."

"How do you know that?"

"Because I read it and then I prayed about it."

"And God answered your prayers?"

"Yes."

"I've been reading Stephanie's copy."

"What do you think about it so far?"

"I'm not sure."

She put her hand on his. "It is true."

Just then Stephanie burst onto the scene. "You two are history! Take that!" She fired an imaginary gun at them both.

The next day Craig went over to be with Rachel while she babysat her six-month-old niece. She gave the baby a bath and then brought her in and put her in Craig's arms.

"This is practice for when we have our own baby," she said.

Craig felt awful. "I need to talk to you," he said.

"What about?"

"While you were gone, I went to a keg party with Bucky Stevens. I met a girl there. We've gone out a few times."

Rachel looked at him. "You're not seeing her now, are you?"

"Yes. I went out with her last night."

"How could you be seeing another girl behind my back after all we've promised each other?"

"I know. I should've told you when you first came back."

The baby started fussing. Rachel went over and took her from Craig. "Do you want us to break up?" she asked.

"No, not really. I just need a little time to figure out what I want." He paused. "The girl is a Mormon."

"And you met her at a keg party? I thought Mormons didn't drink."

"Most of them don't."

"But she does?"

"Yes, but she's trying to quit. I've been reading a book she loaned me. It's called the Book of Mormon."

"How do you feel about her?"

"I'm not sure. I really like being with her. Of course, I like being with you too, but in a different way. I'm not sure what to do, but I thought you ought to at least know. Maybe we should start dating other people for a while, like our folks want us to do."

With tears in her eyes she walked out of the room. He went home and told his parents. Then he called Stephanie and asked her to go out with him on Friday night.

The rest of the week passed quietly. Stephanie limited her drug and alcohol use to lunch hours and at night in her room. Jessica paid for most of it because Stephanie's source of easy money was gone. "You're going to have to find a way to help pay for some of this," she said on Thursday.

"Like what?"

"Start dealing."

Thursday night after roadshow practice, Stephanie tried to figure out what to do. She knew that becoming a drug dealer was a big step. After thinking about it for a long time, she finally decided the best thing she could do would be to get off drugs altogether, and so on Friday she didn't go over to Jessica's during lunch.

She made it through the whole day. On Friday night she went to a movie with Craig.

"I'm quitting everything," she said proudly.

"That's great.

After she got home that night, she went to her room and got ready for bed. She felt restless and panicky. She couldn't sleep. She got up and paced the floor. A few minutes later she went to her closet and grabbed the locked file box where she kept everything and carried it to her bed. She sat on the bed, her legs crossed, and stared at the box. She felt as if her head was going to explode.

"No, not anymore, not ever again," she told herself. Then she returned the file box to the closet and lay down again.

She lay in bed and watched her digital clock mark off the minutes. After ten minutes she sat up. "No, no, no, no, no, not anymore, not ever again, no," she chanted.

At two thirty she slipped out to the backyard and got high on pot. But even as she felt the tension drain away, tears rolled down her cheeks because deep inside she knew she couldn't stop herself anymore.

On Sunday morning Craig stopped at the Bradshaw's to go to church with Stephanie, but when he got there, Kim told him Stephanie had gotten sick at the last minute. So Craig went with Kim and her parents.

It was so different from what he was used to—not as reverent, not as quiet, not as impressive a service, but still, there was something there that he liked.

Stephanie, at home while everyone else was at church, wrote Craig a letter:

Dear Craig,

By the time you read this, I'll have left home. I know it's only a matter of time before I have to get out of this place. The thing is I'm pretty sure I'll never be able to quit using drugs. I've tried and it's too hard for me, so it's only a matter of time before I have to get away from here.

You're the nicest guy I've ever met and I'll always remember the good times we had together. I know you wondered why I insisted that Kim come with us last week. It's because I knew I was going away pretty soon and I kind of hoped I could sort of, you know, give you Kim. That's not exactly what I mean, but I know you'll understand what I mean. The thing is that Kim, even though she's younger than me, is the way I should've turned out. And sometimes when I look at her, I feel so bad because I can see how messed up my life is.

I can't seem to get through a day by myself anymore. It's like there's this monster that's come in and taken over and has to be fed every day.

I'm sorry for the bad example I've been to you. Deep in my heart I know the Church is true. It's just that I can't live the way I'm supposed to. So that's why I'll be leaving some day. Not right away. Just sometime. It might not be for a year. I just don't know. But one thing for sure, I've got to have money to buy the things I need to keep me going. It used to be so much fun, but now it isn't fun anymore.

I'm giving this letter to Jessica because I don't want my mom finding it before I go. I'll tell Jessica to give it to you after I'm gone.

I love you, Craig. You're the kind of guy I'd like to have married if I'd never got into drugs and alcohol. But I can't get out of this mess I'm in and I know I'll never be any good for you. But you'll always be my one true love.

Take good care of Kim for me, even if it's only as a friend.

Love, Stephanie.

P.S. I wrote this letter stone cold sober.

At school on Monday Stephanie waited for Mike at his locker.

"Hi, Stephie, how's it going?"

"How does a person get to be a dealer?"

"You interested?"

"Yeah, I am."

"What for?"

"I need the money."

"To keep you in treats?"

"Yeah."

"No problem. I can get you whatever you need. There's just one thing. You need a safe place for storage. What I've done is to get an outside lock for my room. Think you can swing that?"

"How'd you ever get your parents to go along with that?"

"Simple. I told 'em I needed my privacy."

"Sounds good. Getting a lock should be no problem."

Stephanie faced another interview with her father after school on Monday. "How did it go today?" he asked.

"Okay."

"Did anyone try to get you to drink or use drugs?"

"No. I guess the word's gotten out." She sensed her father expected more than that. "Well, there was one thing that happened—a guy asked me if I wanted to go to a party Friday night."

"Does he drink or use drugs?"

"Yeah."

"What did you say?"

"It was hard for me, you know, 'cause I really do like to be with my friends. I told him I'd think about it."

"What do you think would be the right thing to do?"
She paused for effect. "I guess not to go to his party."
"I think that's right."

"All right, I won't go." She paused. "Instead of that, would it be all right if I slept over at Jessica's house? She's having a few girls over for a slumber party. We'll just watch a few movies and maybe order pizza about midnight."

"Will her parents be there?"

"Yeah, her mom will be there for sure."

"That sounds innocent enough to me. Go ahead."

"Thanks." She stood up. "Oh, there's one other thing. I was wondering if I could get an outside lock for my door."

"What for?"

"Sometimes Kim gets in my closet looking for clothes to wear. And besides, I want to be treated more like an adult, because when I'm at BYU, I'll be living in the dorms with my own key. Also, sometimes I just need a little privacy. I hate to be praying and have Kim come busting into my room."

"I don't like the idea of locked rooms in this house."

"Well, could you at least think about it?"

"Yes, of course, I'll think about it."

"Thanks, Daddy. See you later."

That night as David and Emily got ready for bed, David said, "I think things are going to work out all right with Stephanie."

"Do you?"

"Yes, don't you?"

"I'm not sure."

"She's definitely making progress. She turned down a chance to be at a party where there'd be beer and alcohol. I'm not saying all our problems are over, but I think if we stay close, things'll work out."

"I'm not convinced she's being totally truthful with us."

"How can you say that?"

"It's just a feeling. She's been so convincing in the lies we've caught her in so far. Right now I can't tell when she's telling the truth and when she's lying."

"If she was going to lie, why would she tell me about guys in school offering her drugs?"

"I don't know."

On Tuesday morning David received a phone call from an aide to the governor of South Dakota. "We received your letter about Family Week," the aide said. "The governor has expressed an interest in promoting this in the state. Could you send us some additional material? I sent you a letter today outlining what else we need. One thing I'm curious about is the program you call family home evening."

"I can send you a family home evening manual, if you want. Try it out on your own family and see what you think."

"Sounds good. Look, if we go into this, we'd want to make it as broad-based a program as possible, involving other churches as well as service clubs and city councils. Will you be the one overseeing the state effort also?"

"I don't know. I'll have to ask about that and get back to you."

President Winder told him he would talk to their regional representative and suggest that David be named as the regional Family Week coordinator.

After school on Tuesday, Stephanie walked with Mike out to his car. He opened his trunk and handed her a small package. "There you go."

"Thanks for helping me get started."

"No problem. I know you're good for it. See you tomorrow."

She stopped by the hardware store on her way home and bought an outside lock with a key for her bedroom.

Nobody was home. She got a screwdriver and by following the directions on the package managed to change locks on her door.

She suspected her mother was suspicious and was going through her things every day just to see what she could find. Just to be on the safe side, Stephanie taped the little zip-lock bag onto one of the wooden slats underneath her bed. The bag contained seven grams of crank. The next thing to do was to make up quarter-gram packets and then sell them to her friends at school.

She was now officially a drug dealer.

7

Wednesday morning after everyone had left the house, Emily decided to wash towels. She started on her rounds to the three bathrooms in the house. When she tried Stephanie's door, it wouldn't open. It was then that she noticed the new lock on the door.

She phoned David. "Did you put a new lock on Stephanie's door?"

"No. Why?"

"I just tried to get in. It's locked from the outside. You don't know anything about this?"

"Well, Stephanie did ask me about getting a lock for her door. I said I'd think about it. She must have misunderstood and gone ahead with it anyway."

"Why did she say she wanted a lock for her room?"

"She said Kim sometimes comes in and borrows her clothes without asking."

"That does happen, but most of the time it's Stephanie taking Kim's things. What should we do about this?"

"Wait till I get home, and I'll talk to her about it."

"She might be hiding drugs in her room," she said.

"I don't think so. She's off drugs now."

"How do you know that for sure?"

"Emily, I talk to her every day."

"Maybe she lies to you every day."

"I don't think so."

"What if I call a locksmith to come and open the door?" Emily suggested.

"Stephanie might think that was an invasion of her privacy."

"Whose house is this anyway? We have a right to walk into any room and look in any drawer we choose."

"Calm down. I'll talk to her when I come home. Maybe she misunderstood what I said when we talked about it before."

"I just want to know one thing—who's in charge around here, you or her?"

"I am."

"I'm not so sure I believe that anymore." After she hung up the phone, Emily stared into space, troubled, for a few minutes. Then she picked up the phone book.

Once the locksmith was finished and gone, Emily entered Stephanie's room. She went through each drawer but didn't find anything. *It's got to be here,* she thought. She took off all the covers from the bed and didn't find anything. She opened the lid of the toilet and looked into the water closet but didn't find anything. She got down on her hands and knees and covered every inch of the carpet but didn't find anything.

She lay down on the floor and looked under the bed. She noticed a small plastic bag, removed it, and stood up. Her heart was pounding and her hands were shaking.

The doorbell rang. She got up and looked out the window. It was her visiting teachers. She opened the window and called out, "Just a minute. I'll be right down."

She carried the bag to her room and put it in her purse and then went downstairs and opened the door.

"Were you exercising?" one of the visiting teachers asked as they sat down in the living room.

"No. Why?"

"Your face is so flushed."

"I was just doing some cleaning."

"Well, we won't keep you for very long."

Emily sat and tried to act interested in their visit, all the while the realization slowing sinking in of the deep trouble their family was in.

"What are some of the things you do?" one of the women asked.

"Excuse me, my mind is wandering today. What were you saying?"

"What are some of the ways you and your husband strive to teach your children the gospel?"

She looked at them as if they were speaking a foreign language.

"You know, like family home evening," the other woman said.

"I'm sorry. I can't seem to concentrate. Can you come back again some other time?"

"Is something wrong?"

"I just got some bad news."

"Can we do anything for you?"

"No, I'll be fine in a minute."

The two women got up. "Please call if there's anything we can do."

"Yes, of course."

After they left, Emily went into the kitchen and sat down and tried to think. She thought about calling David but figured he would just say he thought they should talk to Stephanie about it. Stephanie would find some way to get out of it, and David would believe her—and nothing would change.

She found herself thinking about her natural father. It had been a long time since she had thought of him, a man she barely knew, a man who drank too much, someone who'd never been much in the picture but who finally drifted out of her life for good when she was four years old. That was when her mother had gotten a divorce. A year later her mother had married again, an older man, a quiet, gentle man who honored his priesthood. When she thought of her father, it was always of her stepfather.

She'd read somewhere that alcoholism could be passed on from one generation to another. For the first time in her life she felt as if she'd been a carrier of a deadly disease and had given it to her daughter.

She remembered back a few years ago when she'd had her wisdom teeth out, coming home and feeling numb to the pain but knowing it was soon going to hurt very much. That was how she felt now. But she also sensed that the numbness was a gift and she had to take advantage of it while she could. More than anything she feared falling apart and not being able to do anything but sob.

I need to do something, she thought. *I need to get started. What should I do?*

An hour later she approached the information desk of the police department. The officer at the desk looked up at her and figured he knew why a woman like her would come to the police station. "One of your kids lose a bicycle?"

"No. I found what I think might be drugs in my daughter's room. Is there someone who can tell me what it is?"

The man's smile vanished. "Down the elevator to the basement. Across the hall from where you get out of the elevator."

"Thank you."

She had hoped for privacy, but there were three people at desks in the room plus two extra policemen. The men were talking sports while a young woman worked at her desk.

"May I help you?" a man asked.

"I found something in my daughter's room. I need someone to tell me what it is." She pulled the bag from her purse and placed it on the nearest desk. The conversation in the room stopped.

"I can help you," a young woman said, getting up from her desk and coming over to Emily. She appeared to be in her twenties. She was attractive, sensitive, and yet somehow also official. She took the bag into a back room for testing. A few minutes later she returned. "It's crank."

"I've heard of crack before. Is that the same thing?"

"No. Crack is a form of cocaine. Crank is different. You've probably heard of speed, right? Well, crank is like speed, except it's very powerful. The chemical name is methamphetamine."

Emily felt as if the room were spinning. "I'm sorry, but I don't know any of these words you're using. This whole thing is like a bad dream. I keep waiting to wake up."

"I understand. Care for a cup of coffee?" the woman asked.

"No, thank you."

"Don't you guys have something to do?" the young woman said to the others.

The room emptied out.

"I don't know what to do," Emily said softly.

"It's tough being a parent sometimes, isn't it."

"Will you have to arrest her?"

"Not necessarily."

"Stephanie is our oldest. She's always been our pride and joy. She's been an honor student. Nearly straight A's." She sighed. "I don't know why this is happening. Maybe we put too much pressure on her."

"Don't blame yourself. Is your husband currently living with you?"

"Oh, yes. Did you think I was divorced?"

"Not really. How is your husband going to take this?"

"I don't know. We knew she had a problem, you see. We found out because she'd been missing so much school.

My husband was trying to work with her. He thought she was over it. He's a man of great faith, you see, and he thought if he prayed hard enough that God would take it all away, but that didn't happen. I don't know how he'll react."

"Have you talked to him about what you found today?"

"No, not yet. Is it okay if I leave the drugs here with you?"

"Of course. I'll take care of it. We may want to talk to your daughter about who sold her these things."

"What would you do if you were me?"

"If your daughter has been using for a while, I'd consider getting her into an in-patient drug treatment program."

"I don't even know where to begin looking for that."

"There's a girl we were working with about six months ago. She ended up going to a drug treatment center near Minneapolis. The last time I talked to her, she was doing great. At least you could start there."

"There isn't one here in town?"

"There's no in-patient facility here yet. Of course there's AA."

"Oh no, I don't want her down there with a bunch of alcoholics."

"Maybe you should check with the facility in Minneapolis then. I have some information about it somewhere." She rummaged through a drawer and finally came up with the name and phone number. She wrote down the information on a sheet of paper and gave it to Emily. "I also wrote my number at home," she said. "If you need me, just call."

Emily stood up. "You've been very helpful. How old are you?"

"Twenty-four."

Emily's voice caught. "Your parents must be very proud of you."

The woman reached for Emily's hand. "It's going to turn out okay. Call me tomorrow and let me know how everything's going."

Emily went to her husband's office at the college. She talked to his secretary and found out he was in a committee meeting but was expected back shortly. Emily said she'd wait.

Ten minutes later David returned. It was so unusual for her to come to his office that he immediately asked, "What's wrong?"

"I need to talk to you."

They went into his office and he closed the door. "I have a class in a few minutes," he said.

"I found a plastic bag in Stephanie's room. There was some white powder in it. I took it to the police station. They said it was crank. Crank is . . . like speed. It's an amphetamine. The important thing for us to know is that it's an illegal drug."

"Have you talked to Stephanie?"

"No."

"Do you know how long it's been there?"

"Of course not."

"It could have been there a long time. Maybe one of Stephanie's friends hid it there for safekeeping."

"David, why can't you admit your daughter is still on drugs?"

"I'm just saying there are other possibilities."

"Yes, and if Stephanie comes up with another explanation you'll accept it as the truth, won't you."

"Stephanie and I are talking about her problem every day."

"Can't you get it through your head she's lying to you every day?"

"You don't know that for sure."

The class bell rang.

"I need to go teach a class," he said.

"When will you be home?"

"The earliest I can make it is four o'clock."

"We need to decide what to do."

"I know. What do *you* think we should do?"

"I don't know. But one thing for sure, it'll have to be something more than just a priesthood blessing." Seeing the expression on his face, she wished she hadn't said it.

After she left him, she went to the city library, which had phone directories from all over the country. She looked up the names and phone numbers of chemical treatment centers and wrote down the information, then drove home and went to work.

She had been a counselor in the ward Relief Society a few years earlier, and from that she had learned how to organize activities. Everything began with a piece of paper and a list of jobs that needed to be done. This was not much different. After an hour she was functioning efficiently. She prepared a page with columns for information about each treatment center, and as she made each call, she wrote down the costs, period of stay, number of adolescents treated, and success rate.

By the time David came home, Emily had done her homework.

8

Stephanie got home at four thirty. Nobody seemed to be home, so she went to her room. The door was open, and yet she knew she had locked it in the morning.

She lay down on the floor and scooted herself under the bed. The bag was gone.

"Looking for something?" her mother asked, walking into the room.

"No, not really. I just lost one of my sweat socks the other day, and I was just checking to see if it was under the bed."

"Are you ever going to tell us the truth?"

"I don't know what you're talking about."

"I found the bag under your bed. I even know what was in it. It's called crank. Aren't you proud of me? I learned several new words today. The people at the police department were very helpful."

"You went to the police?"

"Yes, of course. That's what they're for, isn't it?"

"I can explain this."

"I'm sure you can. You're very good at explaining."

David entered the room.

"I was just keeping it for a friend," she said. "She wanted me to keep it just for a day." Her parents were staring at her. "Gosh, you don't think I'm using crank, do you?"

No answer. Only stares.

"Look, I've completely given it up. Daddy, you believe me, don't you?"

"I wish I could."

"I've been telling you the truth all along."

"Don't plan on going anywhere tonight," Emily said.

"I'm supposed to go to roadshow practice."

"You'll miss it then, won't you," Emily said.

David couldn't see what would be wrong with Stephanie's going to a roadshow practice. "We'll talk about roadshow practice after supper."

"She's not going anywhere, David." Emily turned to Stephanie. "Supper's ready. We're eating early so Kim can go to the practice."

"I'm not hungry."

"You'll sit with us anyway," Emily said.

"I need to change clothes. Is that still allowed?"

"We'll be downstairs waiting for you," Emily said. "Bring Kim with you when you come."

After Stephanie changed, she went into Kim's room. "Are you the one who told them I had a stash under my bed?"

"How could I? I didn't even know about it."

"Well, that's it. It looks like I'll be cutting out of here soon."

"Where are you going?"

"I'm not sure. Anywhere as long as it's far from here."

"What's going to happen to me?" Stephanie asked, as she finished what little food she'd put on her plate.

"We'll tell you as soon as we decide."

"Don't I have any say about it?"

"No," her mother said.

"I'm through eating. Can I go up and take a shower?"

David and Emily stayed at the table and listened to the water from the shower.

"What is she doing in there?" Emily asked after ten minutes.

"She always takes long showers," Kim said.

"I don't trust that girl. Excuse me please."

Emily went to Stephanie's room and tried the door to the bathroom. It was locked. She went to a hall closet and found the tool they'd had since the girls were children that allowed them to get into a locked bathroom. She worked the tool as quietly as she could. Finally she threw open the door. The shower was running and the blower fan was on, but Stephanie was sitting on the floor, wearing her terry cloth robe. She was smoking.

"How dare you do that in this house!" Emily screamed, grabbing at the joint. "This is marijuana, isn't it?"

"No."

"Tell me the truth!"

"All right, it's pot. I had one more left, and I thought I'd better finish it up or else Kim might find it and try using it."

Emily began pushing Stephanie out of the bathroom. "Get out!"

"I haven't had my shower yet."

"Get out, I said!"

Emily turned off the shower and came out to face Stephanie. "Put some clothes on, and then I'll get your father up here and we'll talk."

"Can't I even take a shower first?"

"Do what I say!"

Stephanie changed.

Emily went to the hall. "David! Get up here right away!"

He came to the foot of the stairs. "What's wrong?"

"This girl has had far too much privacy around here.

I want you to take the doors off her bathroom and her bedroom too."

"What happened?" he asked.

"I caught her smoking marijuana in the bathroom. Take the doors down, David. I mean it."

"I'll have to get some tools," he said. He went to his workshop in the basement while Emily went back into Stephanie's room.

"Where's the rest of it?" she asked Stephanie.

"I don't have any more. That was my last one."

Emily went to the closet. "Is it in here?" She tossed a pile of clothes onto the floor.

"What are you doing?"

"Tell me where you keep it!"

Emily went to Stephanie's chest of drawers and began dumping the contents of the drawers on the floor. "Where is it?"

Stephanie realized her mother would ransack her entire room if she didn't tell her. "It's in that box where I keep my diary . . . in my closet."

Emily dragged the file box out of the closet. "Open it."

Stephanie undid the lock. Emily opened the box and found the bag of marijuana.

David came into the room with his toolcase, and she thrust the bag of marijuana in his face. "This is what your precious daughter does in our home when we think she's taking a shower!"

David looked over at Stephanie. "Is this true?"

"Yes, but I was cutting down."

"Clean up your room," Emily ordered.

Stephanie began putting away the things her mother had thrown on the floor.

"We must have been such an easy mark, weren't we?" Emily said. "Well, those days are over."

David removed the doors and carried them one at a time to the garage. When Stephanie had everything cleaned up, Emily said, "Now come down and help me with the dishes. Come and work for a change. Find out what it's like."

They silently worked in the kitchen. David, his face like granite, walked past them and went into his office and shut the door.

When they finished with the dishes, Stephanie said, "Now what?"

"Go to your room."

"Am I a prisoner here?"

"That's right, you are."

When Stephanie got to her room, she pulled off her bedspread. Then she got some tacks from her drawer and hung the bedspread from the doorpost so she'd have a little privacy.

She phoned Jessica. "My parents found my stash."

"What are they going to do?"

"I don't know."

"You think they'll send you to a rehab?"

"Look, there's no way I'm ever going to a rehab. Can you find a place where I can hide for a couple of days until I figure out a way to get out of town?"

"You can probably stay in my uncle's cabin in Keystone. He only uses it in the summer. Nobody would ever think to look for you there."

"Is that the place where we had a party that one time?" Stephanie asked.

"Yeah."

"That'd be good. Also, do you have any money I could borrow?"

"I might be able to get a little. I know you'd do the same for me."

"Thanks. I'll call you back when I find out what's happening."

"Tomorrow I'll be at school all day."

"Thanks. See you later."

She hung up the phone. It was perfectly quiet in the house. She walked down the hall. She could hear her parents talking in the kitchen, so she crept down the carpeted stairs until she was just outside the door to the kitchen.

"The man I talked to in Minnesota said he thought our insurance would cover it," her mother was saying to her father. "He recommended we bring her in right away."

"It's seven hundred miles. Do you want me to go with you?"

"Can you get away?"

He paused. "Well, I do have classes tomorrow."

"I can make it by myself. I think I'd better not start until morning, though."

Stephanie quietly went back up the stairs. She phoned the bus station. A man answered. "How much would it cost to go to California?" she asked.

"What town in California?"

"Los Angeles."

"One hundred fifty-three dollars."

"How much would it cost to go to Denver?"

"Seventy-one dollars."

"Thank you."

She looked in her wallet. She had fifteen dollars. She went to Kim's room. "I need some money," she said.

"What for?"

"To pay a guy back for the stuff Mom took. If he doesn't get paid tomorrow, he's going to send some guys over to beat me up. Help me out with this, Kim, and I'll never ask you for another thing."

"I don't have anything to give you."

"You want me to get beat up?"

"Borrow it from Mom and Dad. I'm sure they don't want you to get beat up."

"Yeah, sure, good idea, I'll do that."

She went to the phone and punched in the numbers.

Craig answered.

"Hi. Guess who?"

"Stephanie?"

"Yeah. How's it going?"

"Not bad."

"Good." She cleared her throat. "Craig, I need a favor. I have to go to Denver tomorrow, and I was wondering if you could, like, give me a ride down there."

"I have to work tomorrow."

"I know, but couldn't you take the day off?"

"What's so important about going to Denver tomorrow?"

"There's a big rock concert there this weekend, and I really want to go to it. C'mon, it'll be a lot of fun. I'll pay for part of the cost."

"My dad really needs me to work for him."

She was desperate. If she couldn't find some money quickly, she'd end up in a hospital with people jabbing needles in her, or else she'd be forced to go through withdrawal. She knew she couldn't face that. Whatever it cost, she had to make Craig take her to Denver.

For days after, she tried to block out what she said next, tried to pretend it had never happened, or that Craig didn't matter much to her anyway. "Think about it, Craig. It'd give us a chance to spend the night together."

There was a long silence on the other end of the phone. At first she thought it was because he was overwhelmed by the idea. But when he did speak, he sounded like a complete stranger. "Do you have any idea how hard it is for me to keep learning about your church when you're such a rotten example?"

She knew she had gone too far. She tried to make it better. "I was just kidding. Really. You don't think I'd go through with it, do you? Really, it was just a joke." She stopped. "The only thing I wasn't joking about is that I've got to leave for Denver tomorrow morning."

"I've got an idea—why don't you ride your broom to Denver?" He hung up on her.

She knew she would have to do it all by herself. Maybe she could hitchhike to Denver before morning. She changed into jeans and a shirt, grabbed her jean jacket and all the money she could find, and started down the stairs.

Her mother was sitting in a chair at the foot of the stairs, reading. "Going somewhere?" she asked.

"No. I just thought I'd get an apple to munch on."

"I'll be here all night, Stephanie."

Stephanie went back to her room and phoned Jessica. She worried about her mother listening in, but it didn't sound like anyone else was on the line. "If I come to school tomorrow, you'd better have some money and a way to get me to your uncle's place. I've got to get away from here. My parents are talking about putting me in a rehab."

"I'll see what I can do."

At nine thirty Stephanie went to her parents' bathroom and looked in the medicine cabinet. She took four of her mother's sleeping pills and went to her room and soon fell asleep.

At seven thirty the next morning her mother came in the room and announced it was time to get up. Stephanie sat up in bed and noticed that two of her suitcases were on the floor of her room, packed but not closed up yet.

"Who packed my things?" Stephanie asked.

"I did," her mother said.

"What for?"

"I'm taking you to a drug treatment center in Minnesota today."

"Don't I have any say in this?"

"No. The clothes you'll wear today are on your dresser. Get dressed."

"Can I take a shower?"

"No."

"Where do you want me to dress? In the hall? I have no privacy at all in this house anymore. Why don't you just invite all the neighbors in to watch while you're at it?"

"Kim's in the shower, and no one else is around. I'll go downstairs and wait for you."

Stephanie got dressed quickly and then went to Kim's room and rummaged through everything, looking for money. She didn't find any.

She went downstairs. Her parents were in the kitchen arguing. She stood outside the door and listened.

"I think we're moving too fast on this," her father was saying.

"David, we have a daughter who's dependent on drugs. How much more information do you want?"

"Maybe we should ask the ward to have a special fast for her."

"I know you think this is a battle between good and evil. And maybe it was in the beginning, when she first made a choice whether to take that first drink. But it isn't that way anymore. Now she's a drug addict and an alcoholic. It's a disease, David. We're now talking about treating a disease. If she had cancer, would you expect it to be cured with only prayer and fasting?"

"No."

"Then don't expect this to be cured that way."

Kim came down the steps. Stephanie followed her into the kitchen and sat down at the table. They had cold cereal and bananas for breakfast. It seemed strange to be eating such ordinary food when this was to be no ordinary day. She wondered if Jessica could help her escape.

"Stephanie, say goodbye to your father and Kim. You won't be seeing them for a while."

Her father gave her a tight hug, then stepped back and looked at her. His eyes were full of anger at having been betrayed and guilt at not going with them to Minneapolis. After a moment, he left for work.

"Be sure and write, okay?" Kim said.

"Yeah, sure. Kim, will you call up Craig and tell him everything?"

"Okay."

"Let's go," Emily said.

Stephanie looked at the clock. It was only eight o'clock. Classes didn't start at the high school until eight thirty. She had to stall, or Jessica wouldn't even be at school.

"I need to go to the bathroom first."

"Hurry up. We have a long drive ahead of us."

She went to the bathroom upstairs, the one Kim used, and locked the door. A minute later she started a shower.

It took her mother thirty seconds to make it up the stairs and start banging on the door. "Get out of there!" she screamed.

Stephanie ignored her. She could always say she couldn't hear over the sound of the shower. A minute later her mother, holding the unlocking tool, barged in the bathroom and demanded that she get out of the shower.

Stephanie took as much time as she could getting dressed again.

By eight forty-five they were getting into the car.

"I need to stop by the school first," Stephanie said.

"What for?"

"To get my books."

"I'll send them to you."

"Mom, c'mon, just let me talk to my friends one last time before I leave."

Her mother hesitated and then said no.

"It'll only take a minute. I just need to say goodbye to a couple of friends."

"I said no, didn't I?"

"Just let me say goodbye to Jessica then."

"No. Get in the car."

They pulled out of the driveway.

9

By eight o'clock that night, they still had a hundred miles yet to go.

"Mom, you look tired. Do you want me to drive?"

"No, that's okay, I'm all right."

"I've been thinking. In a way I'm glad to be getting away. Things were getting so crazy back there."

"I felt like I didn't even know you anymore."

"I know. Sorry."

"I love you, Stephanie. I'd do anything for you."

"I love you too."

Minutes passed in silence.

"I guess I won't be in the roadshow, huh?"

"No, I guess not. I asked Kim to tell Sister Jackson so they could get someone else to take your part."

"Good." She tugged at her hair and then used the soft light from the radio to look. "I'm losing my hair. It must be because of the drugs."

"It'll come back."

"I hope so. Are you going to head back as soon as you drop me off?"

"No. Tonight we'll stay in a motel, and tomorrow morning I'll help you get checked in."

"I'm not sure what to expect."

"Me either. I feel bad about leaving you with strangers. It's just something we both have to get through. They're all set up to help you—that's the thing we have to keep in mind."

They arrived in Minneapolis at ten that night. Emily stopped at a phone booth next to a gas station and called to get directions.

While her mother was talking on the phone, Stephanie saw two men on motorcycles pull up at the gas station. She thought about going over and asking them to take her with them. They would ride during the day and drink at night and she'd be free and nobody would tell her what to do. But then she got a better look at the bikers. They had big bellies and streaks of gray in their beards.

She sighed. It was no use. She was going to a rehab.

They checked into a motel close to Northern Plains Treatment Center, just north of Minneapolis. "Can I call Jessica?" Stephanie asked as soon as they walked into the room.

"It's late. Why do you need to call her?"

"A while back I wrote Craig a letter and gave it to Jessica and told her to get it to Craig in case I left town. I need to tell her not to give it to him."

"Why? What was in the letter?"

"I told him I loved him."

"Do you?"

"Yeah, I think so."

"Why don't you want him to read the letter then?"

"I wrote it thinking I'd be leaving and never coming back. You say things differently to a guy if you know you're never going to see him again." She paused. "And another thing—I sort of gave him Kim."

Emily's eyebrows raised. "What exactly do you mean by that?"

"Nothing really. I just asked him to take care of her, and I said Kim would be good for him."

"Stephanie, honestly."

"I know, it was stupid. But the thing is they would be good together, you know, like in about five years."

"You call Jessica right away."

Emily took a shower. When she came back in the bedroom, Stephanie was talking on the phone. "It's time to get off the phone now," Emily said.

"I've got to go. I'll see you when I get out . . . Yeah, we'll have to do that all right . . . You take care of yourself, okay? . . . Okay, 'bye." She hung up.

"Well?"

"She's already given the letter to Craig."

"Stephanie, that boy is not going to spend time with Kim. She's too young, and he's not even a member of the Church."

"You're right, but if they were to become just friends, you wouldn't have to worry."

"You'd trust him with Kim?"

"Yeah, sure. Absolutely."

"Well, I'm glad you have a friend like that, for you. But from now on, don't give your sister away anymore."

They both started laughing. "You're fun when you're not being a mother," Stephanie said.

They slept until nine the next morning and then had breakfast and drove to the center. Emily parked in the loading zone. "You might as well bring in your things," she said. She glanced at Stephanie. Instead of the usual bluff and bluster, her daughter looked like a scared little girl.

Northern Plains Treatment Center was run like a hospital. They had to fill out forms, and people with name tags asked questions about insurance.

The counselor who dealt the most with teenagers, Joe Adrean, came up to them and introduced himself. He was

102

tall, bearded and bald, a man who, when he was young and living in Chicago, had been heavily involved in drugs.

"This is a forty-five-day program," he explained. "For the first two weeks, there's no contact at all with the outside world. The last week of the program is called family week." He turned to Emily. "We'd like the entire family here for that. After family week, we're through with Stephanie, but I'd suggest you consider having her spend a month in a halfway house."

"Why?"

"She'll need time to get adjusted to returning to the real world again. That's what a halfway house does."

"And then I can go home?" Stephanie asked.

"Yes, and then you can go home."

"Do you have TV in the rooms?" Stephanie asked.

"We don't watch TV here. We're too busy for that. You won't even read anything except what we ask you to read. We have large-group sessions and small-group sessions every day. We break once a day for volleyball, but other than that, your day will be filled with learning activities."

"How many people are my age?"

"Right now you're the only adolescent. But there are quite a few in their early twenties. You can learn from everyone who's here. Come and I'll introduce you to your roommates."

Stephanie's roommates were twenty-four-year-old Allison, thirty-one-year-old Dana, and thirty-eight-year-old Fay.

"I need to search your suitcase now," Joe said.

"What for?"

"To make sure you're not bringing drugs in with you."

He opened her suitcase and went through each item. He handed Emily the music tapes Stephanie had brought. "No tapes. Take this back home." He found a couple of paperback books. "No books." He found a bottle of aspirin. "No pills."

"What about cigarettes?" Stephanie asked, then glanced self-consciously at her mother. "Sometimes I smoke."

"We don't care if you smoke."

"It's an addiction too, though, isn't it?" Emily asked.

"Yes, but if you give an alcoholic something else to work on, he'll work on that instead of getting off alcohol. Besides, smoking isn't in the same league as alcohol or drugs."

Emily was a little disappointed they wouldn't help Stephanie quit smoking too.

After thoroughly searching the suitcase, Joe turned to Emily. "You should go now. Stephanie has a lot of work to do, and she might as well get started now."

Emily reached for Stephanie's hand. "Well, it looks like this is it."

Stephanie looked as if she were going to cry. "Can't you stay for at least one more day, until I get used to everything?"

One look at Joe Adrean, and Emily knew that wasn't possible. "Can she walk me to the car?" she asked.

"Yes, of course," Joe answered.

There was so much to say and no time to say it. "Be sure and brush your teeth."

"I will."

"I also put floss in your suitcase. Be sure to use it."

"I'll have the cleanest teeth of anyone here."

"I forgot to put in toenail clippers for you."

"I'll borrow somebody else's."

"I'm not sure if head lice is a problem in a place like this, but if it is, write and let me know. I can tell you how to get rid of it."

"I don't think it'll be a problem."

"Just one more thing, the most important of all. Some of these people may tell you there's no God, but I want you to know that your mother knows that Heavenly Father loves you very much." Emily stopped. Tears were sliding down her face. "I'm sorry to be rattling on like this, but it's so hard for me to leave you here with all these strangers. I don't know anything about these people. I don't know what kind of morals they have or anything about them. I just wish I could be here with you to make sure nobody hurts you. Oh, my precious Stephanie, you're still my baby. I love you so much. I wouldn't leave you here if I didn't believe it was for the best."

They threw their arms around each other.

"I love you too, Mom."

Finally, reluctantly, painfully, Emily stepped back, got in her car, gave one last wave, and drove away.

Joe Adrean, having watched from inside, came out to Stephanie, who was wiping her eyes and watching the family car get smaller and smaller as it faded into the distance.

"Come on in, Stephanie, and get free."

Emily spent that night at Chamberlain, although she could have made it back to Rapid City in one day. But because of the drive the day before and the strain of what she'd been through the last few days, she couldn't seem to stay awake. After eating, she checked into a motel, took a shower, then phoned David and filled him in on what had happened that day. After that she watched TV for a while. It seemed so strange to be alone with nothing to do and nobody to provide for. It reminded her of when she'd been in college, when the only person she needed to care for was herself.

The next day at noon she pulled into her driveway. Though it was Saturday, nobody was home. She walked through the empty house, mentally checking what had been neglected in her absence. In the bathroom she found the toothpaste out on the counter. In twenty years of married life, she couldn't remember a day she hadn't had to put the toothpaste back in the cabinet after someone had used it.

She could tell David and Kim had at least made an effort to clean up, but they'd missed places. In the kitchen she opened the refrigerator. There was part of a Domino's pizza and, what was more surprising, a box of blueberries. Emily had never bought blueberries in her life because they always seemed too expensive for their budget.

She opened the cupboards. There was a box of Grape Nuts cereal. She usually only bought inexpensive, house-brand cornflakes. Instead of a loaf of bread in the breadbox, she found two packages of pita bread. She never bought pita bread either.

She went upstairs and noticed that David had rehung the doors in Stephanie's room. She went in and sat on the bed. The room seemed empty with Stephanie gone.

At two o'clock Kim came home from the mall, where she'd gone with a friend. She greeted her mother, asked how the trip had been, and then sat down to practice the piano. It wasn't enough for Emily. She came over and sat next to Kim on the piano bench and put her arm around her.

"What?" Kim said.

"Nothing. I just want to be close to you."

"What for?"

"To let you know what a wonderful girl I think you are."

Kim frowned. "Oh."

"I know it hasn't been easy for you with Stephanie running wild the way she was. We're so lucky to have you in our family, Kim. You haven't given us a worry in the world."

"Mom, I really need to get my practicing done so I can start on my homework."

"Yes, of course. You won't ever start drinking, will you?"

"No, not after seeing what it's done to Stephanie."

Emily went out to buy some groceries for supper. When she got home, she put a roast in the oven. David came home about five and explained that he'd been catching up on some work in his office at the college. They sat down to talk.

"What's your overall impression of the place?" he asked.

"They seem to know what they're doing. I wish there were more people Stephanie's age, though. She's really the only one there now, but they say it's always changing."

Not that they would ever admit it to Stephanie, but during that first supper they felt that peace had returned to their home.

"I need to go to a roadshow practice," Kim said. "Jamie is picking me up."

"Did they get someone to take Stephanie's place?" Emily asked.

"Yeah, but everyone's mad at us for pulling Stephanie out at the last minute."

"Do they know where she's gone?"

"I don't know," Kim said.

A car honked. Kim hurried out the door.

"I suppose we'd better go to the roadshow next Friday, since Kim is in it," Emily said to David.

"I need to go anyway, because of it being a stake activity."

"David, on the last week of the program they have what they call family week. We'll need to be there for the entire week. It begins on a Monday and ends on a Friday. And then we'll need to look into finding a halfway house for Stephanie to go to for thirty days." She knew what he was thinking. "I think the insurance will pay for it."

"How could this have happened to us?" David asked.

"I don't know, but what's done is done."

"I can't get over the fact that when I talked to her after

107

school about her day, everything she told me was a lie. She was still using drugs just as much as before. If she'd just told me the truth, I think I could have handled it, but to sit there and lie to me every day . . . "

"She didn't keep using just to get back at us. She did it because she was addicted. She would have lied to anyone."

"What did we do wrong in raising her?" he asked.

"I don't know."

"You've thought about it though, haven't you?" he asked.

"Yes." She considered letting David know her fear that she had passed on from her natural father the tendency for becoming alcoholic, but, like a monster in the shadows, she couldn't bring it out yet for fear it would be too much of a burden to carry. Better to let it lurk in the shadows of her mind.

David shook his head. "It doesn't make any sense. We had family home evening, we had family prayer, we gave her piano lessons, we went to her school plays, we took her to church, and we tried to live a good example. And then all of a sudden this happens."

They had no answers.

That night Emily lay in bed reading a chapter from the Book of Mormon. David came out from the bathroom. "Oh," he said, "something interesting happened while you were gone."

"What?"

"I got a phone call from the governor."

"What about?"

"A while back I wrote him a letter asking him to declare the week of Thanksgiving as South Dakota Family Week. I told him about the family home evening program and suggested he recommend that families in the state adopt it. He called to say he likes the idea and that he wants to do it. This will mean a lot of good publicity for the Church."

"David, that's wonderful. You must be very pleased."

"Yes. The stake presidency was ecstatic when I told them about it." He sat down on the bed. "There's just one thing."

"What?"

"The governor and his aides would like to meet with me next week."

"Oh? Where?"

"In Pierre."

"What about your classes?"

"I don't have classes on Thursday, so if I leave Wednesday after my last class, I can meet with them the next morning and then drive back."

Emily, fighting tears, used the ribbon to mark her place in the scriptures and set the book on the bedstand.

"What's wrong?" David asked.

"Do you have any idea what it was like for me to leave my daughter in the care of strangers? I needed you to be with me, so we could help each other get through it. But you couldn't come because you had classes to teach. All right, I could accept that because that's how you make a living. I had to do it all by myself. But then something like this comes along, something that will make you look good, and you suddenly discover you can 'make arrangements.' You couldn't go with me to take Stephanie to treatment, but you can do this."

"I thought you'd be happy about this," he said.

"Why did you think that?"

"What's gotten into you? I'm just doing this for the Church."

"Would you like to know why I think you're doing it?" she said.

"Yes."

"I think you're seeking refuge in church service so you can escape your responsibilities in your own family. I also think that's why you're considering applying for the po-

109

sition of vice-president. It's so much easier to look good anywhere else but in your own family, isn't it?"

He picked up his pillow and walked out of the room. She knew he'd gone to the guest bedroom. She turned off the light and went to bed, but she tossed and turned and couldn't get to sleep.

Half an hour later he opened the door and asked, "Are you asleep?"

"No."

"Can we talk?"

"All right." She turned on a lamp and got out of bed and put on a robe. "Where?"

"In the kitchen, I guess."

They went to the kitchen. "Do you want me to fix some cocoa?" she asked.

"If you want some, go ahead, but don't fix anything for me."

She felt awkward around him, as though he were a stranger. They faced each other across the kitchen table.

"You're not very happy with me, are you," he said.

"No, right now I'm not."

"What was I supposed to do—tell the governor, 'No, I can't meet with you because I've got a daughter in a drug and alcohol treatment center, and until she gets out I can't do anything because if I do, my wife will get mad at me'?"

"I don't care if you meet with the governor or not. That isn't the point."

"What *is* the point then?"

"David, look, compared to some wives, I know I don't have very much to complain about. I appreciate all you do for us. You work hard and you provide for our physical needs and you carry out your church responsibilities and you live the standards of the Church. I appreciate all of that."

"But you think the only reason I do some things is so I can look good, is that it?"

110

"I'm just saying that when things aren't going very well in a family, it's sometimes easier to go outside the family for success instead of trying to work things out."

"Do you want me to ask to be released from the high council?"

"No, not really."

"What is it you want then? What have I done that's so wrong?"

She sighed, knowing that to go further would hurt him, but realizing it was time to let him know what she was feeling. "It's not so much what you've done, David."

"What do you mean?"

There was a long, painful silence. "It's what you *are*."

There was another long silence.

"I don't know what you mean."

"When it comes to anything emotional, you always pull away. I've told you before that you're very stingy with hugs. I need them all the time, not just when we go to bed. When's the last time you hugged Stephanie or Kim? When's the last time you held my hand in church? Maybe you don't need hugs, but I do, and Kim and Stephanie do too. When's the last time you took a day off in the summer and went up to the lake with us? You're always too busy. There're always more important things to do, aren't there? Well, life is passing us by. What are our children going to remember about you, except that you were always too busy for them and always doing more important things? Why didn't you come with me to Minneapolis? You could have gotten someone to take your classes. Why do I always have to be the one who handles things like this? David, I'll tell you the truth, I get so tired of the lack of emotional support you give to this family." She sighed. "I know you have plenty of complaints about me too. I guess we both have to learn to live with the things about each other we can't change. I'll try to do that with you."

He was stunned as it became clear to him that her

dissatisfaction was much more than his not going with her to Minnesota, that it was much, much deeper. What was so disturbing was that he had thought things had been going along all right between them.

"Write out a list of things you want me to improve on, and I'll start working on them."

"It's not like that, David."

"Why isn't it?"

"Because I know what would happen. You'd have the list done in a week, and you'd think that was all there was to it. You'd go with me to Minneapolis whenever I went. And every day you'd come in and give me the 2.75 hugs you estimated I need every day and then you'd go on to something else, and all the time it'd still just be mechanical with you."

He looked confused. "I don't know what you want me to do then."

"I'm not asking you to change. I've sort of given up on that idea."

"Do you blame me for what's happened to Stephanie?"

"No. I blame myself more than you."

"You? Why?"

She couldn't even say it, not even to him. "No reason, I guess."

"It sounds to me like you've written me off," he said.

"No, not really. I guess I've decided to just be realistic, that's all. You are the way you are, so I might as well try and accept it."

He gave her a cold stare. "Don't do me any favors, Emily."

He spent the rest of the night in the guest room. When he awoke at five the next morning, he made the bed so she wouldn't have that to complain about. He skipped breakfast and went to his six o'clock high council meeting. The stake president announced he needed a high councilor to travel to Belle Fourche to make a change in the elders quorum presidency. David volunteered. After church he went to his office at school and prepared a tentative plan for the state's celebration of family week. By the time he returned home in the early evening, Emily and Kim had already eaten. He piled food on his plate and went to his study to go over the Family Week plans once more. He slept in the guest bedroom again that night.

In the morning as he prepared to leave the house, he found a note Emily had left him. It read, "What are your intentions regarding this family?"

"Thank you for seeing me," David said as he entered the stake presidency office Monday after work.

"No problem," President Winder said. "What's on your mind?"

David sat down. "I think you should release me as a member of the high council."

"Why's that?"

"Well, I'm not sure if you know this, but we've had a lot of problems with Stephanie lately. She's gotten into alcohol and drugs. Right now she's in a treatment center in Minnesota. Emily took her there this week." He sighed. "But that's not all. Emily and I haven't been getting along very well either. To tell you the truth, I'm not sure our marriage is going to survive. I think Emily's sorry she married me."

He stayed with President Winder until seven o'clock and then went home. Kim was practicing the piano when he walked in the house, not playing a song, but pounding away on exercises like a machine. It seemed to have very little to do with music.

"Hi, Kim."

She didn't look at him. "You missed supper. We waited for you to come home. Mom started crying and then went upstairs to her room."

David was sensitive she had called their bedroom Emily's room, but he didn't say anything about it. "I was talking to President Winder."

"You always tell us to call when we're going to be late."

"You're right. I should have done that. I'll go apologize to your mother now." As he left, Kim continued to beat on the piano.

Their bedroom door was shut. He knocked softly.

"Yes?"

"Can I come in?"

"Yes."

He walked in the room. Emily was lying on the bed, a box of tissues beside her.

"I'm sorry I was late. I was talking to President Winder . . . about Stephanie . . . about whether or not he should release me . . . and about us."

He sat down beside her on the bed. "Emily, you've got to let me try to change. You can't just write me off. I can change. I've been changing all my life. I can't stand knowing you're not happy with me."

She sat up.

"I know you're thinking that whatever I do to try and be more what you need won't be natural. Well, you're right. It won't be at first, but maybe it can be, if I practice at it. Maybe I can become more what you need me to be."

"It's not fair to expect you to change just for me. You are what you are."

"But I can change. That's the one thing I've picked up through the years. I know how to learn."

"It's not just you, David. I have such a long ways to go too."

"I love you, Emily."

"I love you too."

They held each other for a long time, and then he excused himself and went to the city library and checked out *Loving Each Other* by Leo Buscaglia. When he got home, he sat down—not in his office but in the kitchen—and read.

That night, at Emily's request, he returned to their bedroom. The next morning things seemed better for them both.

10

On the first day at the treatment center, Stephanie was given a complete medical exam. She also took a test called the MMPI. The person in charge kept asking the same questions over and over in a slightly different way each time. She couldn't understand how he could find anything out about her from that.

On the second day she sat for the first time in what was called Small Group. It consisted of six people and a counselor. She listened as members of the group told intimate details of their lives. She couldn't relate to anything they were saying. They were so much older than she, and the problems they had were more serious, even overwhelming. That, plus feeling awful as she went through withdrawal, made it so she hated being there.

After three days of Small Group, she went to Joe Adrean. "I've got to call home and talk to my mom."

"What for?"

"Just let me talk to her, okay?"

"All right. Go ahead. You can use this phone." He left her alone in his office.

Emily answered.

Stephanie sounded desperate. "Mom, you've got to get me out of here."

"What's wrong?"

"These people are all alcoholics and drug addicts. One man is fifty-two years old. He got drunk every day for twenty years and ended up losing everything. One woman used to be a prostitute in Minneapolis because of drugs. Another woman started drinking when she was a nurse in Vietnam. Mom, I'm sixteen years old. I didn't start heavy drinking until this year. All I did was drink and skip school a few times. What am I doing here? This is all a big mistake. At least get me to a place where there's somebody my own age. Mom, Mom, please," she sobbed, "you've got to get me out of here. I can't stand it anymore. It's so depressing being around these people all the time. Please, I'll do anything you ask, but get me out of here."

"Let me talk to Mr. Adrean, will you?"

Emily shared her misgivings with Joe. She ended with, "I've decided to come for Stephanie and take her home."

"Before you do that, I'd like you to talk to one of our medical staff. Hold on a minute and I'll switch your call."

After a brief pause, a woman answered.

"Mr. Adrean asked me to talk to you about my daughter," Emily explained. "Her name is Stephanie Bradshaw."

"Oh yes, just a minute." A long pause. "I have her file now. What's your question?"

"I've made a mistake putting my daughter in your program. I'm going to come and get her."

"I wouldn't advise that. We tested Stephanie yesterday, a psychological test. What it does is to test anger levels. In addition, we medically tested her for alcoholism levels. What we've found is quite alarming. The quantities your daughter has been drinking are lethal. Basically she has two options—she can get treatment or she can die."

Emily was stunned. "There must be some mistake."

"No, there's no mistake. I know this must be a shock to you."

"But she's only sixteen."

"The earlier a child begins drinking, the more quickly it becomes deadly. There's a basic rule we use. If an adult drinks every day but doesn't use other drugs, it will take about five and a half years to become an alcoholic. For an adolescent it takes about five and a half months. For a pre-adolescent it may take as little as five and a half weeks. Stephanie began when she was twelve. She is now on the brink of death."

"Are you absolutely certain?"

"Yes. Would you like me to transfer you back to Mr. Adrean?"

"Yes, please."

Joe picked up the phone. "Any more questions?"

"How can your program help a sixteen-year-old girl when there's nobody around for her to relate to?"

"Well, that's a good question, and I wish there were more kids here right now. One thing about adults in this program, though—they're here because they've hit bottom and want to climb back out of the hell they've created for themselves. Teenagers who enter a program like this usually come because of their parents. They're not as motivated as the adults. But I think some of the adults' drive to straighten up their lives can rub off on the younger ones. To be honest, there are some good arguments for getting Stephanie into a program that deals only with adolescents. If you are set on getting her into an adolescent program, I can give you the names and addresses of some excellent ones. They're usually filled up, but you're sure welcome to try."

Emily was still reeling. "I'll look into the other programs, but for now I guess we'll leave her with you. Can I speak to Stephanie again?"

Joe handed Stephanie the phone.

"Mom, when are you coming to get me?" she asked.

"I've decided for now we're going to leave you there."

"No! You can't do that! Mom, please, you've got to

118

come and get me! I won't ever drink again. I promise. Just don't make me stay here."

"It's for the best. We'll come and visit you soon."

"No! I can't stand it here! Mom, please . . . "

Joe took the phone. Stephanie was crying so hard he had to speak up to be heard. "Mrs. Bradshaw, if there's nothing else, I'll say goodbye now. Look, we'll keep you informed on how Stephanie is coming along. Okay?"

"Okay."

"Fine. Goodbye then. Call me anytime you want."

On Friday evening David and Emily went to the road-show at the ward. Some members of the ward, mostly youth, were upset at them for pulling Stephanie out of the roadshow at the last minute. Others who had heard about her being sent to a drug rehabilitation center didn't know what to say. A few were secretly critical of the way David and Emily had raised her. They were the ones who told each other confidentially, "They wouldn't have had any problems with her if they'd just . . . "

The young men's president came up to them. "Too bad Stephanie won't be in the roadshow tonight," he said. The "too bad," instead of being consolation, was used as a weapon. He was still furious with them for ruining his production. Stephanie, even at her stoned worst, was better than anyone else he could replace her with.

"Thank you for your concern for our daughter," Emily said, responding on purpose to his words rather than his tone of voice.

Later, as she thought about that night, Emily realized how sensitive she and David were. If people passed them without speaking, to them it meant rejection, but in reality it might mean those individuals had other things on their minds, or that they had not even heard about Stephanie. Some did know, of course, but didn't know what to say, and so in reality they did avoid talking to David and Emily.

Emily didn't want advice on what she'd done wrong in raising Stephanie, nor did she want glib solutions. All she needed was for her friends to tell her they'd heard about Stephanie's problem, and that they were sorry, and was there anything they could do to help.

Some had done that on the night of the roadshow. A man and his wife who had had problems with their own children came up. The woman looked took Emily's hand and asked, "How are you doing?"

"We're doing okay. Thank you for asking."

The husband, a car mechanic by trade, rested his hands on David's shoulders. "If we can do anything for you folks, just let us know."

"Or even if you just want to talk, give us a call," the woman added.

"Thank you so much," Emily said.

Just before their ward's production began, the director came out. "I just want to thank Michelle Roberts for filling in. She learned about this just a couple of days ago, and she's really done a good job. Let's give a big hand for Michelle!" Everyone clapped.

"Stephanie is a nonperson now," Emily whispered.

"What are you talking about?"

"Just wait and see. Nobody is going to mention her name. If she had cancer and couldn't be in the production, people would go out of their way to pay tribute to her."

"What's that got to do with it?"

"Alcoholism is a disease just like cancer."

"There's a difference. You don't choose to get cancer. You do choose to become an alcoholic. That's a big difference."

"Some people are predisposed to becoming alcoholics. It's not a choice they make."

"They choose to take the first drink though, don't they?"

"David, Stephanie made the choice to take that first

drink when she was twelve years old. *Twelve years old.* How could she know then how disastrous a decision that would be in her life?"

"If she'd just lived the way we'd taught her, she would have escaped all this."

"We can't live our lives on what-ifs. We have to deal with reality."

"Where did we go wrong?" he asked.

"I don't know. I don't know anything anymore."

"Me neither."

David, feeling awkward and uncertain, concerned about their marriage, reached out and held Emily's hand through much of the evening.

When the roadshow competition was all over, their ward did not win.

The next day Emily went grocery shopping. When she came back, Craig was in the driveway talking to Kim.

Emily gave him a cold reception. "Kim, you have homework to do, don't you?"

"I've got it all done."

"Hello, Mrs. Bradshaw."

"Hello, Craig. I guess you know about Stephanie, don't you?"

"Yes."

"It's too cold to be outside."

They agreed and followed her into the house.

Emily sat in the kitchen and brooded that Craig was talking to Kim in the living room. She also wondered what he thought when he read in Stephanie's letter that she'd given him Kim.

She decided this was war.

A few minutes later she took a tray of food in for them. "I thought you two would like a treat," she said.

"Milk and cookies?" Kim said.

"You know how much you like milk and cookies, Kim."

She turned to Craig. "She always has a glass of milk and a cookie when she comes home from school. She's been doing that since she was in the first grade. It seems like just yesterday." She set the tray down. "Kim, why don't you have Craig quiz you on questions from the driver's manual?" She turned to Craig. "She'll be getting her learner's permit in a few weeks. I bet that brings back memories for you, doesn't it, Craig?"

"Yeah, right."

"Well, you two have a nice chat." Emily left the room.

"I don't know what's wrong with my mom," Kim said. "She's so weird today."

Craig smiled. "I think she's trying to protect you from me."

"It's so embarrassing. What do you think we should do about it?"

"Nothing. I need to go now anyway."

"I'm still not sure why you came by when you knew Stephanie was gone."

"Stephanie asked me to check up on you once in a while, that's all."

"You talked to her since she left?"

"No, she sent me a letter."

Emily came bouncing into the room. "Don't mind me. I just need to water the plants."

Craig couldn't let a golden opportunity like this go by. "Mrs. Bradshaw, Kim and I have a question for you. Do you happen to know of any states right around here where a girl under eighteen doesn't need permission from her parents to get married?"

"What?" Emily cried out, spilling water on the carpet.

Craig started laughing. "Sorry, it was just a joke."

Emily was furious. "That's not something to joke about."

"I'm only here because Stephanie asked me to check and see how Kim is doing."

"She also said she thought that you and Kim could be . . . uh, close."

"Oh, *that*. Mrs. Bradshaw, Kim is real fine and I like her a lot, but she's more like a kid sister than anything else. I'm not about to start chasing fifteen-year-old girls. Things aren't that desperate for me yet. Look, if you don't want me to come around here anymore, just say so."

Emily felt that Craig was telling the truth, but she also felt it would be best if he were out of the picture until Stephanie came back. "Maybe that's what we should do."

"Fine, no problem." He stood up. "Oh, there's one other thing. Stephanie loaned me a book about your church. I can go home and get it now if you want me to, but if you can wait a few days, I'd appreciate it. I'm almost through with it."

"You are?"

"Yes."

"Oh."

Craig walked toward the door. "Well, I'd better go. Kim, if you ever need to talk, give me a call."

"Wait," Emily said. "Do you have any interest in learning more about the Church?"

Craig thought about it. "Yeah, I guess I do."

"Let me talk to the missionaries and see about having you over to listen to them. They have a series of lessons they give. You might enjoy it."

"It doesn't have to be here if you're uncomfortable about me being around Kim."

Emily thought about it. "No, it's all right. Now that we've had a chance to talk, I understand things better."

And so everything was resolved. The only difficulty was that Kim began to fantasize that when she got older, she and Craig might get serious. That possibility made boys her age seem immature and not worth the effort of paying any attention to them. She also spent a lot of time trying to figure out ways to look older.

123

11

Once a day Stephanie went to Large Group, where they were taught about chemical dependency, how to express feelings, what it means to level with someone, and how to be more self-assertive. They were given a number of handouts and asked to study them.

She also went twice a day to Small Group, where individuals could express their feelings and talk about things in their past. Stephanie mainly listened to others and learned about their experiences.

After several days in Small Group, she was asked to talk.

"What about?" she asked.

"Whatever you want."

"I don't have anything to say."

"Tell us why you're here."

"It's all a big mistake."

"You're saying you don't have a problem. What have you used?"

"Well, a little beer on the weekends, but everybody my age does that."

"What else?"

"Well, a little pot, and crank, but just a few times."

An older man broke in. "A little of this, a dab of that.

If you can't level with us, why don't you just keep your mouth shut?"

She glared at him.

Joe Adrean spoke. "He has a point. I think you're minimizing your problem."

"I don't have a problem."

"Then why are you here?" Joe asked.

"My parents overreacted, that's all."

The man couldn't take that. "You know what I think? I think you're a brat who's always gotten her way. You're not doing anything to help yourself. If you ask me, you're selfish and self-centered."

One of her roommates broke in. "And while we're on it, I'm getting fed up watching you check off each day on the calendar. Why are you even here if you aren't going to do anything?"

"Look, it wasn't my idea to come here, okay? Besides, I'm not like you people. I'm not an alcoholic and I'm not a drug addict. So quit treating me like one."

"What do you think an alcoholic looks like?" Joe asked.

"Alcoholics are old men who stand on the street and beg quarters."

"And drug addicts?"

"They're people who shoot up. I've never shot up."

A woman said, "Wake up and smell the coffee, gal. You're an alcoholic and an addict, just like the rest of us."

"No, you're wrong. You're all wrong."

"Maybe you and I could talk about this afterwards," Joe said.

"Fine, but it won't change anything. I'm still not an alcoholic."

Joe Adrean met with Stephanie after lunch in his office. "I'm going to ask you some questions," he said, "and I'd like you to be truthful, okay?"

"All right."

125

"Are most of your friends people who drink or use drugs?"

"Yes, but that doesn't prove anything."

"Wait a minute. You don't have to be so hostile, do you? I mean, after all, what can I do to you, send you to a rehab? Hey, you're already here. So why not try and take advantage of what you can learn while you're here? How about just leveling with me? You might as well. There's nothing I can do to you, either way, whether you tell me the truth or not. But maybe you'll learn some things about yourself if you're honest with me. Okay?"

She thought about it for a long time. "All right."

"I want you to imagine something very wonderful has happened to you, like maybe you've won a brand new car, or a vacation trip to Australia. What would you do if that happened?"

"Go out and celebrate."

"How would you celebrate?"

"Go party."

"I see. Okay, now I want you to imagine that something very bad has happened, like . . . let's see . . . suppose a guy you were very much in love with told you he wanted to break up. What would you do to help you get through that?"

"Go get drunk."

"So with either good news or bad news, you'd go get drunk."

"Yeah. So?"

"Nothing. It's just something to think about. How good would the good news have to be?"

"What do you mean?"

"What's something you celebrated that really wasn't all that wonderful a thing to celebrate?"

"Every week we used to celebrate Hump Day, you know, Wednesday. It means the week is half over."

"And how bad would the news have to be to cause you to want to get drunk?"

"Mondays."

"You'd drink because it was a Monday?"

"Yeah, sometimes."

"Sounds like you drank a lot. Let's talk about that for a minute. Before you came here, how often were you using drugs or alcohol? Was it every day?"

"No, not every day."

"How often? Once a week, or once a day?"

"It wasn't every day."

"You missed some days then?"

"Yes."

"How many days during a week would you miss?"

She thought about it. "At least two days a week."

"So at least two days a week you didn't have anything."

"That's right."

"What two days would that usually turn out to be?"

"Well, for one, Sundays usually."

"Why Sunday?"

"Because I had to go to church with my parents. And after church I usually caught up on my sleep. There was nothing else to do."

"So you didn't use at all on Sunday?"

"No."

"Not ever, by yourself?"

She hesitated. "Well, sometimes, after church, when I took a shower, I'd get high."

"In your house?"

"Yes."

"With your parents there?"

"Yes."

"I don't see how you could get away with that."

"I have my own bathroom. I turned on the shower and used the fan to blow the smoke out of the house."

"So sometimes you did use on a Sunday?"

"Yes."

"Was that every time you took a shower then?"

"Not every time."

"Most every time?"

"I guess so."

"So on some Sundays you actually were using. Is that correct?"

"Yes, I guess so."

"And what was the other day during the week you were thinking of when you told me you didn't use every day?"

"No particular day."

"What would a day when you didn't use anything be like?"

She cleared her throat. "I don't understand the question."

"Would it be a school day or a weekend?"

"A school day."

"Would it be a day when you didn't take a shower?"

She looked trapped. "No."

"You took a shower every day then?"

"Yes."

"And almost every day you took a shower you got high?"

"Yes."

"So, if you think about it, you really were using every day, weren't you?"

She looked down at the floor. "I guess so."

"I think that's very interesting, don't you?"

"I could've stopped any time I wanted to, though."

"Are you sure about that?"

"Yes."

"In the last two months, how many days have you gone without using anything?"

"I can't remember."

"Well, have you gone a week without using within the last two months?"

"No."

"Have you gone three days without using anything?"

"No."

"Have you gone two days without using anything?"

She brought her hand to her mouth. "No," she said quietly.

"Let me ask the question over again. In the past two months have you gone one whole day without using anything?"

She sighed. "No."

"Does it surprise you to realize how much you were using?"

Her voice could hardly be heard. "Yes."

"Have you ever stolen anything to get money for drugs or booze?"

"You mean like at a store? No."

"Have you ever taken money from someone in your family to get money for drugs or alcohol?"

"No."

"You never did?"

"No."

"And yet you were using every day. How could you afford it?"

"My friends paid for a lot of it."

"Can you think of a time in the past two months when you needed money for drugs or alcohol?"

"Yes."

"What did you do?"

She cleared her throat. "I used my mother's bank card."

"And you don't consider that as stealing?"

"No. She said I could use it."

"Did she know you were using her money for drugs and alcohol?"

"No."

"Do you think it would have been okay with her that you did that?"

"No."

"If she knew about what you'd been doing and I came up and asked her if you ever took money to buy drugs and alcohol, what do you think she'd say?"

"She'd say yes."

"So you have stolen money to support your habit."

"I guess so."

"Have you ever skipped school to go drink or use drugs?"

"Yes."

"In the past two months how many times do you think that would have been?"

"I don't know."

"More than once a week?"

"No, not that often."

"The week before you came here, how often was it?"

She shook her head. "That week doesn't count."

"Why doesn't it?"

"Because my parents were out of town, so we did it every day until they got back."

"How many days was that?"

"Three days."

"And before that?"

"I usually didn't skip the whole day. A lot of times it was just in the afternoon."

"We'll count more than two class periods as one day."

"That's not fair to count it that way."

"I just want to know, in a given week, how many times would you leave school unexcused to go party?"

"Two or three. Usually every Friday because it was TGIF day, and a lot of times on Wednesdays, because it was, you know, Hump Day."

"You celebrated the middle of the week and the end of the week, right?"

"A lot of times we did."

"And on Monday you drank because it was the beginning of the week?"

"Yes."

"That's three times a week you were skipping at least two class periods, right?"

"Yes."

"Have your grades gone down in the past year?"

"A little."

"What kind of grades were you getting a year ago?"

"Mostly A's."

"What grades will you be getting on your next report card?"

"Mostly D's and F's."

"That's more than just a little then, isn't it?"

"Yeah, it is."

"Well, all right, let's change the subject. Have you ever bragged about drinking somebody under the table?"

"Yes."

"You can hold your liquor then?"

"Yeah, sure."

"Does it take more beer now to make you feel good than it used to?"

"I can handle it better now."

"So you drink more now than you used to."

"Yeah, sure. When I first started, a couple of cans was all I could handle."

"Now how much does it take?"

"I don't sit there and count."

"Can you drink a six-pack all by yourself?"

"It depends on how much time you give me."

"Well, say in a couple of hours, could you drink a six-pack?"

"Yeah, but that's not so unusual. A lot of my friends do that too."

"Have you gone on to other drugs?"

131

"Yes."

"What?"

"Crank, but I didn't shoot up."

"You snorted it then."

"Yes."

"Let me ask you a question. What difference does it make how it gets into your body?"

"Drug addicts shoot up."

"What are you saying—that because you didn't shoot up, you're not a drug addict?"

"That's what . . . " She paused. "That's what I used to think."

"Now what do you think?"

She stared at the floor.

He was sensitive to the turmoil she was going through. "Stephanie, now what do you think?"

"I'm not a drug addict."

"What other drugs have you used?"

"Quaaludes."

"What else?"

"Ecstasy."

"What about cocaine?"

"No."

"You've never used cocaine?"

"No."

"That's interesting."

"Why?"

"Because we found traces of cocaine in your body the first day you came here."

"Oh. Well, I used it just a couple of times the week my parents were gone."

"Just a couple of times?"

"I swear that's the truth."

"I see. Here's another question for you. Have you ever been a drug dealer?"

"I was just getting started at it before I came here."

"What made you want to sell drugs?"

"I needed the money."

"Why did you need the money?"

"Because my parents took away my mom's bank card."

"You needed the money to support your drug and alcohol use?"

"Yes."

"Thank you. One more question. You don't have to answer this unless you want to. Have you ever offered to have sex with someone to support your drug and alcohol use?"

"No." She paused and then in agony closed her eyes.

"You're thinking about something though, aren't you?"

"When I figured out my mother was planning to send me to a rehab, I asked a friend of mine to take me to Denver. He didn't want to so I told him that if he would, I'd spend the night with him. But I never would have. I would have talked him out of it once we got to Denver."

"But you did make the offer?"

"Yes."

"What did he say?"

"He told me to go fly my broom to Denver."

"He called you a witch?"

"Yes. I don't know if he'll ever talk to me again. He was one of the nicest guys I've ever met. We got along so well the first time we met. It was like magic. So I really messed up major with him."

"Stephanie, I think we're about finished here. I'd just like to summarize what we've talked about. The picture I'm getting is of a person who drinks and uses pot almost every day, who takes someone else's money to pay for her habits, a person who in the last two months hasn't gone a day without using something, a person who's lost interest in everything, including school, except drugs and alcohol, a person who is moving on to hard drugs, a person who has become a drug dealer to support her habits, a person who would do almost anything to protect her drug and alcohol usage. Now if someone were to come up to you and describe a person like that, what would you say? Is that person an alcoholic and a drug addict or not?"

She stared at the floor.

"Stephanie?"

Tears were threatening to come. "Can I go back to my room?"

"Yes, of course, if you'd like to."

For the next two days she didn't say much of anything, but then on the third day in Small Group she said, "I have something to say."

"What is it, Stephanie?" one of the group asked.

"I'm sorry I've been such a pain to you guys. I've thought a lot about it, and now I know you guys were right. I am an alcoholic and a drug addict."

The ones who had been the hardest on her came over and hugged her.

That was, for her, an important turning point. But there were many more yet to come.

12

Stephanie probably received more letters in treatment than anyone else there. This one was from Kim:

Dear Stephie,
   Hi! How are you? Hope it's okay there. Don't worry. I'm not mad at you or anything. But hear me out or write me out. Ha! Ha!
   I have sent a piece of gum and the flavor will last about as long as the love of the people who gave you drugs. See you soon. Love you a lot.
                                      Love, your sis,
                                      Kim
P.S. Write soon if you can.

Another letter was from Craig:

Dear Stephanie,
   A few days ago Jessica gave me the letter you wrote before you left. I'm glad that deep down you really do believe the things you've been taught in your church.
   Don't worry about what you said when you wanted me to take you to Denver. I knew it wasn't you talking, that it was because of the drugs. Don't worry about it. Your family says you're doing good and that they can hardly wait to drive out and see you.

I've started listening to the missionary lessons at your house. I'm really enjoying it. So thanks for loaning me your book. Oh, I finally returned it to your parents after the missionaries gave me my own copy.

Kim's been sitting in on the missionary lessons too. She really knows a lot about your church. We're getting to be good friends. She's like a kid sister to me.

Sometimes I think about what it will be like when you come home. We had fun before, but I think we could have a lot better time staying away from alcohol and drugs. Maybe when you get back we can get together again. I think about you all the time.

Love,
Craig

This letter was from Emily:

Dear Stephanie,

Well, we are trying to adjust to having you away. Our weather has been a little warmer lately. I notice our temperatures are higher than yours. We are looking forward to seeing you as soon as they'll let us. How are you doing? I pray for you constantly and think of you many times a day. I love you very much and have great faith in you and your ability. I know that you are very important to your Heavenly Father and that he is very interested in what you are doing.

Tonight Daddy took us out for Chinese food and Kim got sick—poor girl.

Craig is doing so well with the missionary lessons. I wouldn't be surprised if he got baptized soon, if his parents will let him, that is. I don't think they're very happy about him learning about the Church.

Dad has some good news. Before you left he wrote the governor and asked him to declare the week before Thanksgiving as South Dakota Family Week. Well, he's decided to do it. The stake presidency has asked the high councilor from Pierre to work with the governor and his staff. In the meantime your father has a new assignment on the high council. He will be the one asked to help improve all the meetinghouse libraries in the stake.

I will close for now. We are really looking forward to our visit.

> I love you lots.
> Always,
> Mom

The first letter Stephanie received from her father was, unlike most of the others she received, printed on computer paper from his office at home:

Dear Stephanie,

Your mother and I love you very much and we miss you. But if this experience will help you, then we should all be thankful.

Right now I'm looking at a report card with all F's on it. That's not the Stephanie I know. I encourage you to make use of the resources there. The people are not likely to be perfect, but I believe they do care. Mom and I care, but we really haven't known what to do to help you once again become the winner that you have always been. It seems that the plan is to help us to change our own attitudes and actions to help us to be a happier, more successful family. I hope you'll accept the love I have for you.

We're really looking forward to seeing you on visitor's day.

We are praying for you in our family prayers and individually. I know the Lord will be there for you when you need him.

I know you're trying to change. I just want you to know that I'm trying too. I'm trying to be more open and warm and loving. I've been reading lots of books about showing love and trying it out whenever I can. For example, you remember Professor Moss, don't you? He's taught in the Math Department for thirty years. The students call him the Monster. Yesterday I walked up to him in the office and put my arm around him and asked him how the best math teacher in the country was. He looked at me like I was crazy. But I noticed that whole day he was more pleasant to others than I'd ever seen him.

I've also been trying to be more openly affectionate with your mother and Kim. Poor Kim, she doesn't know what to make of it. At first I could feel her tense up when I hugged her and told her how much I loved her, but yesterday she came over and hugged me for no reason at all.

It's not easy for me to change, just as I'm sure it's not easy for you, but sometimes we all have to do things that are hard. I guess that's how we grow.

Your loving Dad

She got a letter from her friend Dana:

Stephie, babe!
You really missed a party last week. We went to a party at a hotel. It was some guy's B-day. I drank sooo much and smoked sooo much weed and did a little cocaine. I spilled my jungle juice and passed out in it and stained my friend's white shirt. Anyway we went back to her house around 6 a.m. and slept all day. It was sooo much fun. We're all just waiting for you to come back.
Take care,
Dana

She also received a letter from Jessica:

Hey Woman!
Thanks for calling me the night before you went to the rehab. Don't worry, you're not missing any real great parties! We're waiting till you get back!
Dean's way in the past now. Me and Jason were going out, but now he's going out with Jennifer. Do you know her? She's a skinny freak! She's cool though. Anyway her and Jason are going

to prom! On prom night I'm going to be home watching a movie and eating Captain Crunch!

Everyone misses you! I still owe you and Megan a night out! We'll go out as soon as they let you back into the real world! Which I hope is soon! Megan told me about a person who got their canary stoned.

So, do you want to know what's going on? Jeff broke up with Kate. Christy Johnson thinks she's pregnant. Amanda and Dana are ignoring each other because Amanda can't smoke for a while and when Dana smokes around Amanda, it tempts her. Kate is trying out for drill team.

Have fun with the cute guys there!

                                    Love,
                                    Jessica

The next Sunday was Fast Sunday.

Emily sat in the congregation while the sacrament was passed and tried to sort out her feelings. She had always felt like one of the stalwarts in the ward, someone who could be counted on to help out in any project. She had served in a variety of leadership positions in the ward and in the stake. She had always been concerned about the ones who "needed help." And now for the first time she was one of those people, and it was hard to get used to.

She had been visited by the Relief Society president and the Laurel class adviser, each wanting to know what they could do to help. It was embarrassing to know that in presidency meetings Stephanie was being discussed. In her worst moments Emily imagined what people were saying. "I hear they had to send her away for drug rehabilitation. She's an alcoholic and a drug addict. I'm not surprised. I could see it coming. Emily and David put too much pressure on their kids . . . "

In some ways she felt betrayed, not by the ward, but by a feeling she'd had that if she did all the things she was asked to in the Church, her children would escape having

139

serious problems. Of course she had seen families with problems and she had even said that "none of us are immune from problems." But deep down she always felt there must be something they had not done.

The fact that Stephanie had not escaped somehow opened up a world of fearful possibilities. If this could happen to Stephanie, what about Kim? Would she turn to alcohol and drugs too? What about premarital sex? Or shoplifting? Or anorexia? Or Satanism? And what about David? Some men, apparently in the best of condition, have heart attacks and die. If it happened to others, what guarantee did she have that it wouldn't happen to them?

Suddenly, as never before, the world was a scary place.

As soon as the bishop turned the time over to the members for bearing their testimonies, Emily walked up to the stand and turned to face the congregation. "I just wanted to let you know how things are going," she began. "For some of you who aren't aware, my daughter Stephanie is an alcoholic and a drug addict. She's in a drug and alcohol treatment center in Minnesota. She'll be there for six weeks and then we'll transfer her to a halfway house. I just wanted to tell you that we really appreciate your prayers and concern very much."

She paused. "It's hard for me to accept the fact that no matter how hard I've tried to do a good job as a mother, it hasn't been enough. When I was younger, I thought I could be perfect in raising my kids. I was critical of others whose children made mistakes. A number of times I've said to others that if these parents had just had family home evening and lived the gospel, they wouldn't have the problems they're having now. And here I am now, in the same situation as the parents I was so critical of. To tell the truth, I don't know what we did wrong. I don't even know what I'd do differently. After all these years I find I don't know anything. Isn't that a joke on me?

"I apologize for the times I've been too quick to judge

the pains that some of you have had to bear. Too quick to say that if you'd just done this, or done that, then you wouldn't have had any problems. I will never do that again. Not ever again in my life. I can see now how true it is that none of us are immune from problems.

"I just want to close with one more idea. I have so much more respect for our Father in heaven than I've ever had before. I'm grateful that he can allow us to come to the earth and learn from our mistakes. What impresses me so much now is that he never gives up on us. I know that God hasn't given up on Stephanie. And because of that, David and I never will either.

"Stephanie won't be perfect when she comes back, but she'll be trying harder than ever before. One thing I'm sure of now, Father in heaven loves her. We love her too. I say these things in the name of Jesus Christ. Amen."

Emily made her way back to her seat and sat next to David, who reached out and squeezed her hand.

After the meeting was over, several women came up to Emily and hugged her.

David had a high council speaking assignment in Hot Springs the next Sunday. A few days before, Emily asked if she could go with him. Kim arranged to spend Saturday night with a friend in the ward so she could go to church with them.

David's talk was different from any Emily had heard him give before. His usual approach had been to find an area he was doing well in and talk about that. But on that day, instead of berating members for not being as good as he thought they should be in some minor area, he tried to give comfort and hope to those who faced difficult problems. He closed his talk with a quote from the Book of Mormon: "And if men come unto me I will show unto them their weakness. I give unto men weakness that they may be humble; and my grace is sufficient for all men that humble themselves before me; for if they humble themselves before me, and have faith in me, then will I make weak things become strong unto them."

On the way home they listened to music. She sat and looked at him.

He noticed. "Something wrong?"

"You're the most wonderful man in the world." She knew he would brush it aside. "I'm serious."

"You didn't think that a few weeks ago."

"I never doubted your integrity." She paused. "I'm grateful you've tried so hard to change. You're more warm and loving and involved in the family than I ever thought you could be." She touched his sleeve. "It's not fair that you should be the one to do all the changing. I've never asked you what you'd like me to work on."

He looked over and smiled. "I like you just the way you are."

"I'm sure you can come up with something."

"Not really."

"Think about it though, will you? I'm serious."

There was, in spite of their getting along better now, a great sadness in her that would not go away. She could push it back some days, but even so it was lurking somewhere in her mind, ready to come out when least expected. It was the possibility that, because her father had been an alcoholic, she was the one responsible for Stephanie turning to drugs and alcohol.

It was the one topic she avoided talking about.

13

The next week Stephanie received another letter from Jessica:

Hey woman! How's it going? Are you doing okay? I
hope so! Guess what, I got suspended from school!
I'm suspended for the rest of the school year. I
never thought I'd get suspended! I guess I messed
up major. But Mrs. Blake is such a witch! Well
maybe it was worth it. You and I had so much fun
together anyway, didn't we? We'll do it again when
you get back.

Remember that night we went to that fraternity
party? Remember that guy I danced with? Well he
came by my house last night and said he wanted to
see me again! I about freaked out! He's my dream
come true!

So, when are you coming back? Take care of
yourself. You better write me back!

Love ya!
Jessica.

Her friend Megan also sent her a letter:

Stephanie,

Hey! How's it going? I'm in 2nd period. We're
supposed to be writing a paper about "The Lord of
the Flies." I got your address from Jessica last

night. We all miss you a lot! I think you're probably just as lucky not to be here. Jessica got kicked out of school and she's just sitting home doing nothing. And I'm in all this trouble at home. My parents are sending me to this stupid shrink and he put me in a group with other teens with problems. But their problems don't even compare with mine. Theirs were like being depressed about boyfriend breakups, low grades in school, talk back to parents. I mean it's like for rich kids. Group don't make no difference cuz I'm still using. I got a 1.4 GPA on my report card so now I can't drive for 9 weeks.

My mom is driving me crazy. I mean she doesn't trust me for anything anymore now. She is always searching my drawers and purse. I wanted to tape a tape from my brother's friend. It's Metallica. Now my mom is all "No, no I have to listen to it first and if I don't like it then no you can't tape it." And I know she won't like it just to make me mad. And we were going to have a party in foods class and I had no money. So I asked to borrow some so I could get some donuts and stuff and she's all "Well I have to go with you to buy it cuz I don't trust you with money. You will probably just go buy drugs with it." That made me so mad. Adults are so messed up. If that's the way she's going to be maybe I should get out of here. I mean she's really overdoing it. I can't do anything now. And Brian broke up with me about two weeks ago. At first it didn't click that we were really broken up but now it hit me and it really hurts cuz I loved him so much and I lost him over drugs. But he came over Sunday. He got a new car, a 67 Mustang, it's pretty bad. But we really didn't talk. I still really like him.

Well, I gotta be going! I miss ya!
Love ya,
Megan

She read the letters from Jessica and Megan in Small Group a couple of days later.

"Why are you wasting our time with this drivel?" a man asked.

"I don't know what to do when I get back. These are my friends. I really like 'em."

"Throw 'em a kiss and get away. That's what you gotta do."

"That's easy for you to say that because you don't have any friends."

"Get outa town. Man, I've got plenty of friends."

"What I mean is, friends aren't as important to you as they are to me."

"That's because you're a ding-y teenager," he teased.

"And you're a dirty old man."

"Can we skip the insults?" Joe Adrean said. "Do any of the rest of you have any advice for Stephanie?"

A young woman in her mid-twenties nodded. "If you go back to your friends who are using, you'll end up using too. It happened to me the first time I went through treatment. I was about your age then, maybe a little older."

"I don't see how I can give up my friends."

"You want to stay sober?"

"Yes."

"You think you can be at a party with your friends, where they're using, and you're drinking soda pop? Forget it. It'll never happen. Oh, it might happen the first time or the second, but eventually you'll start in again too."

"That's not true. Besides, none of you know how important my friends are to me."

"All right," Joe said, "why don't you tell us about your friends?"

"When we were together, we could just be ourselves and not worry about what anybody thought. I mean, I didn't have to be perfect around them. They just accepted me for what I was."

"Did they accept everybody in the same way they accepted you?"

145

"Yeah, pretty much."

"Even the ones who didn't drink or use drugs?"

She thought about it. "No, but those people wouldn't have wanted to be with us anyway."

Joe looked at her and nodded. "So what you're saying is that in order to be accepted by this group, you pretty much had to drink and use drugs."

Stephanie felt like a trap was being set. "Not necessarily."

"All right. Was there anyone in your group of friends who didn't drink or use drugs?"

Stephanie looked down.

"Did you hear the question?" Joe asked.

"Yes."

"Let me ask it again. Was there anyone in your group of friends who didn't get drunk and use drugs at least once a week?"

"No."

"So what will happen if you go back to your old friends?"

She slumped down in her seat and covered her face with her hands.

"Are you all right?" Joe asked.

"I'm just thinking, that's all," she said.

It took Stephanie a long time before she realized she couldn't take up with Jessica and her other friends when she went home.

A new patient was called a junior peer. Every new patient was assigned a senior peer whose job it was to guide and orient the new patient through the treatment process.

Stephanie's senior peer was Marta Olsen, who was twenty-six years old. She took her role seriously and met with Stephanie almost every night just before bed.

"Have you read 'Three Factors of Addiction'?" she asked one night.

"Yeah, sure. It was only two pages long."

"Can you remember what the three factors of addiction are?"

"Let's see. One has to do with the fact that it can run in your family."

"Right. That's physiological. Does it run in your family?"

"Not that I know of."

"What's another factor?"

"They talked about how movies and TV ads and everything make it seem like you'll be really popular if you drink."

"Good. That's what they call social custom. You're doing great. What's the third one?"

"I can't remember."

"It's called self-medication of needs. That's if you use alcohol to numb or quiet emotional or physical pain, or even if you're using it to help you overcome shyness or being lonely. Does any of that describe you?"

"No, I don't think so. I'm not very shy usually."

"I've noticed that. Just kidding. Is there any emotional pain you're trying to hide?"

"I don't think so."

"Sometimes when a teenager gets into drugs and alcohol in a bad way, a lot of times there's been sexual abuse early in her life."

"That's not the case with me," Stephanie said.

"Good. I just wanted to check. It was with me. It took me twenty years before I talked to anyone about it. It was like a sore that was festering for all those years and I didn't even know it. I just wanted you to know, if it was a problem with you, that it's best to get it out in the open."

"Thanks, but I'm okay on that."

"Just checking. Great."

147

Another letter came from Craig:

Dear Stephanie,
I've started to go to church activities with Kim.
I really enjoy them. There's a girl there I'd kind of
like to take out, just until you get back, of course,
because after you get back I want to spend a lot of
time with you. Her name is Tara. I knew her in
high school a little. She's graduating in June and
then she's going to BYU. I've seen her a couple of
times at church and we've talked on the phone a
couple of times.
Maybe you can help me. The thing is, I'm
afraid of what Kim will think if I start going out
with Tara. Kim sort of goes around like I'm her
property. She's a nice kid and everything, but not
someone I could ever get very serious about. I
mean, come on, a guy has to draw the line
somewhere, right? I figure a girl I date should at
least be legal to drive a car by herself after eight
o'clock at night. One thing though, Tara's a nice
substitute, but nobody's as much fun as you are.
Kim keeps talking about how much your dad is
changing. She says he hugs her and tells her how
much he loves her practically every day. Last
Friday your parents went away together to a motel,
just the two of them. Kim couldn't handle that. She
kept saying how old they were to be acting like
that. Personally I think it's great. To me it's like
your dad is trying so hard to be what you need him
to be when you come back.
My mom is getting real critical of me taking the
missionary lessons. Two nights ago she had me
visit with Father Anderson about the Mormon
church. He wasn't very complimentary. I guess
maybe he feels threatened. I told him that the
things he was saying weren't true.
Your family is all excited that they're going to
be able to see you this weekend. I wish I could
come along, but I know this has to be a time with
just your family.
I'm sending along with them some cookies that

Tara and I made for you today. I hope they're not
too bad.

Love,
Craig

"No reason not to make a bit of a vacation out of it,"
David said as they pulled out of the driveway Friday at
noon on their way to visit Stephanie.

It was, however, nobody's idea of a vacation — a twelve-
hour drive that ended at one in the morning on Saturday,
when they checked into their motel room in Minneapolis.
Kim wanted to swim, but the pool was closed after ten
thirty. She wanted to watch TV, but her parents said she
needed to get some sleep.

They slept until eight and then had breakfast before
driving out to the rehabilitation center.

At the desk they asked for Stephanie. A few minutes
later she came running down the hall and threw her arms
around her mother first and then her father. Her father
would hardly let her go. It seemed so odd to her.

"Oh, gosh, it's so good to see you guys," she said.

"You're looking good," her father said.

"I feel good too. Thanks for sending me here. I feel
like I've really come a long way."

She turned to the woman at the desk. "These are my
parents. I'll be going out with them all day. Joe said you'd
have something for us to sign."

The woman gave her father a form to sign.

As they walked to the car, Stephanie filled them in on
what was happening in her life. "This past week I started
going to AA meetings," she said. "That's the thing that'll
keep me on the straight and narrow. One of their meetings
each week is for people my age. It's so great! It's like the
Church in a lot of ways. It was so great to be with people
my own age again. And I could really relate with a lot of
the things that some of them said. When I get home, I'm

149

going to really get involved in AA. They say that if you go to at least ninety meetings in ninety days, you're probably going to be able to stay sober. I think it'd help you guys too if you'd start going to Al-Anon. There'll be some people there who've been through the same things you're going through."

David drove them over to the motel and they ate lunch. Then they all went swimming, even her dad, which was unusual for him. After half an hour, their parents had had enough and went back to the room. Stephanie and Kim got in the hot tub and soaked.

"So, how are things going with you?" Stephanie asked.

"Okay."

"You and Craig getting along?"

"Craig's going with Tara now."

"He's not actually going with her, is he?"

"He spends more time with her than he does with me."

"You really like him, don't you."

Kim blushed. "Not really."

"C'mon, you can tell me the truth."

"I wish I were your age—then I'd at least have a chance."

"I'm glad you're not, 'cause if you were my age, I wouldn't have a chance. I mean, all I'd do my whole life is take phone calls for you. I think it's better this way. By the time I'm out of the house, it'll be all one phone can do to keep up with your calls."

"Oh, sure."

"I'm serious. Gosh, Kim, don't you know how foxy you are yet? I'll tell you the truth, I'd trade bodies with you any day."

Kim looked to make sure Stephanie was serious, and when she was convinced she was, she got a big smile on her face.

Two college guys looked in the swimming area, saw Stephanie and Kim there, and decided a swim was just

150

what they needed. A few minutes later they returned, dressed in their swimming trunks, and came over to the hot tub.

"Need a little company?"

"Yah," Stephanie said with a Swedish accent and a big smile.

They sat down, one next to Stephanie, the other next to Kim.

"You two from out of the country?"

"Yah, ve're foreign exchange students from Sveden. Ve're coming to learn about America, yah?"

The two guys grinned. "Hey, we'll teach you."

Stephanie looked over at Kim. She was giggling.

"What's so funny?" one of the guys said.

"She doesn't speak much Anglish, but she tinks you're very handsome, no?"

"She does?"

"Yah, I tink so."

"Would you two like to come up to our room for a drink?"

Stephanie pointed to the water they were sitting in. "Vhy go dere ven dere's so much vater here, no?"

The two guys laughed. "But we can get you very good drinks in our room. Whatever you'd like."

"You have carrot yuice, yah?" Stephanie asked.

"Carrot juice?"

"Yah, it's vhat ve drink in Sveden."

"Sure, we can get you carrot juice . . . somewhere. No problem."

"And you have maybe . . . pickled herring, yah?"

"We can get pickled herring."

"Ve'll have some party den, yah?" she said.

"You got that right. What else would you like?"

"In Sveden, ve go so crazy for pickled pigs' feet." She turned to Kim. "Is dis not true?"

Kim was laughing so hard she could only nod her head.

"Dat one dere especially gets crazy ven she have pickled pigs' feet. See, she get crazy yust tinking about it."

"We'll be right back with some!"

"Ve be here vaiting, and den ve have such a party, yah?"

The boys nodded and ran out to their car.

Stephanie and Kim giggled all the way back to their room. Their parents knew something was up but couldn't imagine what it was. The girls each took a shower and then watched a movie on TV and then it was time for supper.

"Would you rather have supper here in the motel or somewhere else?"

"Somewhere else!" Stephanie and Kim both said in unison.

After supper they took Stephanie back to the treatment center. Kim wanted to see Stephanie's room, so the two girls went up while David and Emily waited in the lobby. Stephanie showed Kim around and introduced her to everyone on the way.

"Gosh," Stephanie said as they went back to the lobby, "I wonder what those guys did with the pickled pigs' feet. I bet they're somewhere out in their car, cruising around, looking for girls. And every time they pull up alongside some girls, the dopey-looking guy, the one I sat by, sticks his head out the window, you know, real cool, and he goes, 'Hey, my buddy and I here have some pickled pigs' feet. You want to have some fun?' "

They both howled with laughter.

"I yust get so crazy vhen I have pickled pigs' feet," Kim said, and then she started giggling all over again. Their parents stared at them in amazement.

The next morning they all went to church and then took Stephanie back and said their goodbyes and started home again.

Ten days later Stephanie got another letter from Craig:

Dear Stephanie,

Guess what, I got baptized today!

My folks finally gave me permission. They weren't all that thrilled with the idea, but my dad said it was my life, and if that's what I wanted, he'd back me on it. Your dad was the one who baptized me. And Kim played a song on the piano. Your mom gave the opening prayer. I felt so good when I came out of the water. It's been the greatest thing that's ever happened to me.

I'm thinking about going on a mission. The missionaries say I should go as soon as I can. If I do, I'll have to postpone college because I don't have enough money saved up for both. I'm thinking about it. I haven't talked to my folks yet. They won't be very enthusiastic about the idea.

Tara and I are going out next Friday. I hope that's all right with you. She's really been helpful to me lately. Her parents are having me over for supper after church tomorrow. She told me her dad is a counselor in the stake presidency, but I guess you know that already.

I just wanted to thank you for being the first one to get me interested in the Church.

More than anything I wish you could have been here for my baptism. Kim came up and gave me a big hug and told me it was from you, but it would've been a lot better coming from you.

Well, I've got to get to bed so I can get up for church tomorrow. I'll be given the priesthood tomorrow after sacrament meeting. I wish you could be here for that.

Love,
Craig

A day later she got a letter from Kim:

Dear Stephanie,

I guess you already know Craig got baptized.

He said he'd write and tell you. I'm glad about it but I'm not glad about what else is happening.

You've got to get back here soon before Tara takes Craig away from you. I'm serious! She makes me sick the way she's playing up to him. Like in fast and testimony meeting, the way she talked about knowing him in school and always thinking he'd make a good Mormon, and how happy she was the first time she saw him in church. She makes me so mad!

If you can hurry through there any faster, then do it, because she's treating him like some prize she's just won.

Hurry up and get back here!

Love,
Kim

Two days later she got a letter from Tara:

Dear Stephanie,

Craig asked me to write and see how you were doing. He talks about you all the time. Actually I should have written anyway because I'm the Laurel class president, so in a way I'm kind of responsible for you anyway. By the way, did you get the cookies? Are you still alive?

I hope you're getting along okay. I saw a movie on TV a while back about this drug addict and so I know it must really be hard for you not to be able to get your fix anymore. But I think where you are is the best place for you right now.

I want to thank you for helping to fellowship Craig. He's such a wonderful new member of the Church. We're all doing what we can to make him feel welcome.

We'll be glad when you come back. Maybe you could give a fireside on drugs sometime.

Your friend,
Tara

She also got a letter from Jessica, in response to a letter Stephanie had sent a week earlier:

Hey Babe!

What do you mean, you're not going to party with us anymore? You sound like they've brainwashed you or something. Or are they reading the letters you send out, so you have to put a lot of garbage in you don't really mean? I mean, what's the deal here?

You know you'll party with us. I mean, what else is there to do? You can say what you want, but we all know you'll be doing it with us as soon as you get back.

How are the guys there? If you don't want to make the censor blush, you can tell me when you come home!

Jessica

14

Family week began on the Monday of the last week of Stephanie's stay at Northern Plains. Her family left for Minnesota after sacrament meeting on Sunday and arrived at their motel at eleven that night.

On Monday morning Joe Adrean announced the final event of the week. "On Friday we're going to have a special meeting," he said. "Each member of the family will tell three things they dislike about someone in the family and three things they like. We're all together in this, so we'll all hear everyone else's comments. We'll give you time to work on this throughout the week."

Of all the things Emily was asked to go through, she dreaded that last day, knowing her family would be opening themselves up for others to see. They each spent considerable time working on their list of likes and dislikes. So that they could express their feelings more accurately, they were each given a list of "feeling words."

Much of what took place that week was worthwhile. The information on building self-esteem and learning how to express feelings seemed like something that might be covered in a priesthood or Relief Society lesson.

The family-list meeting began on Friday at ten in the morning. Those who took part were the ones who, like

Stephanie, were in their last week at the center. Everyone sat around in a circle, and the two people involved in giving and receiving the list of likes and dislikes sat on chairs in the middle of the circle.

The Bradshaw family's turn came at three o'clock.

"Stephanie, who do you want to start with?" Joe asked.

"My dad, I guess."

"All right."

David came up and sat down. One of the rules was that the two must sit facing each other, knees touching.

Stephanie looked down at her notes, gulped, and began. "I know you've been trying to change," she said, "but I'm going to talk about things I didn't like when you were the way you used to be. I hated it that no matter what I did in school, it was never good enough for you. One time I brought home four A's and a B, and all you did was ask me what went wrong in the class I got a B in."

She paused and glanced down at her notes. "I hated having to go with you when you had to travel to another ward to speak. It was like we were supposed to be perfect little angels all the time. It made me feel like it never really mattered to you what happened as long as I put on this big front that everything was all right.

"My last one is I don't like it that you were always working and never had any time for fun. It made it so if somebody in the family wasn't working, we were made to feel guilty."

"David, do you have your list for Stephanie?" Joe asked.

"I do." He looked down at his notes and then at Stephanie. "I feel frustrated that from the time you were born we tried to teach you to stay away from alcohol and drugs. If you'd just followed what we tried to teach you, none of this would have happened.

"Second, it makes me mad when I realize how much you've used us. You've lied to us, you've stolen money

157

from us, you've violated the trust we had in you." He reached out and held her hands in his. "With all my heart I hope there will come a time when I'll be able to totally trust you again.

"Number three: Did you have an accident in the car while we were gone and then tell us that someone must have hit you in the airport parking lot?"

"Yes."

"It makes me angry to know you'd do that to us. What did we do to you to be treated in such a manner?"

Tears formed in her eyes. "I feel ashamed for having done that."

"Whatever happens from now on, no matter how bad it is, don't lie to us anymore. I think I can take anything now, but not being lied to."

There was a long silence. "Do you have your list of likes for each other?" Joe asked.

Stephanie nodded and pulled away so she could look at her list. She wiped her eyes with a tissue and then began. "Daddy, I appreciate you coming here this week. I know it meant you had to leave your work. Also, I like it that when you first found out about my drinking and everything, that you tried to work with me so I'd quit. I like it that you try and do what's right for the family and that you haven't given up on me yet."

He nodded and reached out again for her hands. "I know it hasn't been easy being all alone here. I appreciate the fact that you've stuck it out and have tried to gain as much as possible from your experiences here. And I'm glad you haven't rejected everything we tried to teach you. Things could have been a lot worse. Also, I'm glad you got Craig interested in the Church. He's been a positive influence in our home while you've been away. Being able to baptize him was a great experience for me. Finally, I just want to tell you how much I love you. I don't think I've ever said that as much as I should have."

158

Stephanie leaned over and hugged him.

Emily was the next to share her lists. She sat down in the chair facing Stephanie, with her knees touching Stephanie's.

Stephanie went first. She glanced down to her paper, cleared her throat, and finally said, "I hated the way we always had to do things for appearances. You wouldn't ever let me wear the clothes I wanted to wear to school. Sometimes I kept clothes in my locker and changed after I got to school just because I couldn't stand to look the way you wanted me to look.

"Also, I hated it when you used to talk about me going to BYU and being married in the temple, like I didn't even have any choice about it. I think you should have asked me if I had any interest in those things, instead of just assuming I'd follow along in your footsteps. I always had the feeling you didn't approve of anything I did — the music I listened to and the movies I watched.

"And I hated that every time I went out, I had to lie to you about what I'd done. Craig doesn't have to do that. He can tell his parents anything, but I never could, because if I told you some of the things I'd done, you wouldn't have been able to handle it. I hated the fact that my whole life was a lie, and neither you or Daddy knew what I was really like. I think right now you and I are pretty much strangers. But I don't want to stay that way. I want to be able to talk to you about anything."

"I want that too, Stephanie."

Stephanie looked down at her paper and continued. "This is my list of likes. I like it that you're the one who made all the arrangements to get me here. And that you drove me out here and that you haven't ever given up on me. And that you send me cards and letters all the time. They really mean a lot to me."

There was a long pause, and then Joe asked Emily to run through her list.

Emily sat with her back straight, her arms folded neatly on her lap, but at the same time, tears were rolling down her face. Using her notes she began. "First, I dislike it that you used my bank card to buy drugs with. I trusted you with that card." She sighed. "We've worked so hard to set aside a little money for you and Kim to get an education, and by the time this is all over, the money will probably all be gone. All my life I wished I could have finished college, and here you are with the opportunity there for the taking, and you're throwing it away. I'm sorry but I just can't understand it."

Stephanie broke in. "What you and Daddy wanted is a perfect little toy wind-up daughter."

"You don't have to be perfect, but a little common decency would be helpful. How could you violate our trust by smoking pot in our house? That still makes me so mad to know that was going on in our home." She paused. "I'll read my list of likes now too. I like it that you've worked hard in treatment. I like it that you haven't run away from here and that you let me bring you here in the first place. And I like it that you're willing to go to a halfway house for another month so you can make the adjustment back to the real world." She paused. "I guess I'm done."

"Kim, I guess it's your turn now," Joe said.

Emily returned to the circle as Kim came up and sat down.

"You two need to have your knees touching," Joe said.

Kim scooted her chair forward a little.

"Stephanie, do you want to begin?" he asked.

Stephanie drew a deep breath before speaking. "Kim, you were the only one in the family that really knew what was happening." She glanced down at her notes. "I'm ashamed I wasn't a better example for you. I'm embarrassed you were the only one who really knew what I was like. I used you, and that wasn't right. Since I've been here I've learned that I forced you into playing a role. You had to be the Hero Child. That means you had to be super good to make up for me. And I forced you into a role of enabling me to keep on drinking and using drugs. I feel ashamed for having used you the way I have."

Kim nodded.

Stephanie continued. "This is my list of likes. I liked it when we played 'Pig's Feet' with those guys that one time you came here with Mom and Dad to visit me. That was like the first thing we'd done together for a long time. I liked the letters and cards you sent me while I've been here. And I liked it that you tried to warn me about Tara making her move on Craig. Also I like it that you tried to get me to stop and that you put up with a lot from me right before I came here. And that you always set a good example for me."

"Kim, do you have your list ready?" Joe asked.

Kim looked down at her piece of paper. "I don't know if I should say this or not."

"I think you should say it if it's the way you feel."

"All right." She read what she'd written. "I hate it that Stephanie is the queen of this family, and I'm the little mouse servant." She looked up. "Nobody pays any attention to me. All we ever do is worry about Stephanie. Well, what about me? Aren't I important?"

"We love you, Kim," Emily said from the edge of the circle.

"What you mean is you're glad you don't have to pay any attention to me. I'm tired of trying to pretend that everything's all right. Everything's not all right with me. I'm always the one nobody notices. When Stephanie comes back, I know we'll all have to be careful what we say or else Stephanie will get mad and go out and get drunk. Stephanie, you're my sister and everything, but in some ways I wish you would never come back home again. I'm all mixed up. Before Stephanie left, I used to sit in my room all alone. I felt so awful but I couldn't tell anyone because I'm not supposed to be the one with the problems. That was Stephanie's job. Just give Kim a pat on the head and tell her what a nice girl she is. That's all you have to do. Nobody really cares about me. Not really."

She slumped over and began to cry. Stephanie got out of her chair and knelt down beside her, and they embraced and cried together. And then Emily came over on the other side and hugged Kim. David joined them and put his hand on Kim's shoulder. None of them cared anymore who was watching.

15

That night they left Minnesota on their way to Colorado to Mountain Top, a highly rated adolescent halfway house. The plan was for Stephanie to stay there for thirty days and then return home.

They stayed the night in a motel in Chamberlain. There was a pool, and even though it was after pool hours, Stephanie and Kim went swimming, hoping to find two guys they could talk into going out to find them some pickled pigs' feet, but nobody showed up. When they returned, their parents were in bed with the lights out. Stephanie turned on the TV and flipped from channel to channel until they found the movie channel. There was a horror movie. "Let's watch this," she said.

"Don't stay up too late," Emily called out.

"We won't."

They turned the TV on low and sat on the floor with their backs up against the bed.

Half an hour into the movie, Stephanie whispered, "How about a pizza?"

"It's too late," Kim said.

"Too late for who? Us? No way. Scrounge around for some money and I'll see what I can find, and then let's go phone from the lobby."

They looked in the yellow pages and called a pizza delivery place.

"You always get what you want, don't you," Kim said.

"What's wrong with that?"

"Nothing. I wish I was more like that."

Fifteen minutes later their pizza arrived. They took it into the room. The smell gave them away. "What are you two doing now?" Emily sleepily asked.

"Eating pizza," Stephanie said.

"It's too late for pizza."

"Not for us," Kim said, giggling.

"Don't wake your dad."

"We won't."

Emily went back to sleep.

Stephanie and Kim sat on the bed, their legs crossed, eating pizza and watching TV.

"This is just like when we were kids," Kim said.

"Yeah, right. Look, Kim, I'm sorry things got so bad when I was using."

"I know you are. It's okay."

On July 5, two weeks after taking Stephanie to the halfway house, Emily received a call from the director. "You'll have to come and get your daughter."

"Why?"

"She got drunk last night."

There was a long silence. "She did?"

"Yes. She went out with one of the others here. We're throwing them both out."

Emily spent most of the day on the phone trying to find a halfway house that would take her daughter. She called all over the country. Nobody wanted her, either because they were already full or they didn't want to deal with a teenager who'd already been kicked out of another program.

She kept putting off calling David and telling him what

had happened. She kept hoping she would at least have made other arrangements before she had to tell him the bad news.

At five thirty he came home.

"What's for supper?" he asked.

"Something's come up."

"What?"

"Stephanie started drinking again. They're throwing her out of the halfway house."

"How could she do that now, after all she's been through?"

"She went out with a guy, and I guess the two of them decided to start up again. I've been trying to get her in another program, but nobody will take her on such short notice."

"Maybe we should just bring her home."

"She's not ready to come home yet."

He sighed. "Maybe she never will be."

"Don't say that."

"You've got to at least think about it as a possibility."

"I have, but we've got to do whatever we can to help her."

He sighed. "You're right. What do you want me to do to help out?"

"If you and Kim can take charge of dinner, I'll keep phoning."

"Where's Kim?"

"Upstairs in her room."

He went upstairs. Kim was talking on the phone.

"Kim, can you help me? Mom's busy."

"Stephanie's been kicked out, hasn't she."

"Yes. Will you come with me to the store and help me pick out something to eat?"

They drove in silence at first. Finally David said, "Kim, if you ever start drinking, I don't think I'll be able to stand it."

"I won't start."

David thought some more. "I shouldn't have said that. If you start drinking, we'll deal with it too, just like we have with Stephanie, because you're just as important to us as she is. But as a matter of advice, I'd suggest you not ever start."

She smiled. "Thanks, Daddy, for saying it that way."

By the time they returned with food for supper, Emily had found another halfway house that dealt primarily with teenagers.

"Where is it?" David asked.

"Salt Lake City. I'll leave tomorrow."

"Let me come with you."

"You have classes."

"I'll get someone else to take them."

"Are you sure?"

"I'm sure."

Tears filled her eyes. "Thank you, David. I would have been all right going there, but I dreaded coming back by myself."

A few days after her arrival in Utah, Stephanie had a talk with a peer counselor, a girl her age, someone who had been through many of the same experiences. Her name was Jennifer, and she was a Mormon too.

"Why'd you start drinking again?" Jennifer asked.

"I don't know why. It was a dumb thing to do. I let everybody down."

"Who'd you let down?"

"My mom and my dad. You should have seen them when they came to get me. They looked so old all of a sudden." She sighed. "And I let my little sister down. All she's ever wanted was for me to get off drugs and alcohol."

"Who else?"

"I let down Joe Adrean. He was a counselor at the rehab I went to."

"Who else did you let down?"

She thought about it. "A guy."

Jennifer smiled. "A guy? You got a picture?"

"Can I trust you?"

Jennifer laughed. "No. See, the thing is, you're stuck here. I can get on a plane and in a couple of hours be making my move on your man."

Stephanie showed her a picture of Craig.

"That does it, I'm out of here," Jennifer teased. "He looks good."

"I think he looks a little like Tom Cruise. What do you think?"

Jennifer looked more carefully at the picture. "Better than Tom Cruise."

"I agree. I've been going crazy knowing he's running around in South Dakota and I'm here in Utah. He just got baptized, and this girl in our ward, she's all, 'Oh, can I help you?' He's dating her now. He says she's just a friend, but I'm going out of my mind sitting around here when I should be home."

"Well, let's get you out of here then. Who else did you let down by breaking the rules at your last halfway house?"

Stephanie thought about it. "I can't think of anyone else."

"What about yourself?"

"Oh, yeah, sure."

"Who were you getting sober for? If it was for anyone else except yourself, it's no good. You got to stay sober for yourself first of all. Not for your mom or dad or your sister or Craig. For you because you're the one who has to live with yourself if you mess up. Nobody else does."

Stephanie thought a lot about that over the next few days, and in time it became very important to her.

Stephanie continued to receive letters. This one came from her mother:

Dear Stephanie,

I hope where you're at has air conditioning because I've been watching how hot it's been in Utah lately. We're not doing much better. Yesterday it got up to 109. This has been the hottest summer we've ever had. It seems like every day breaks a record.

How are you doing? Just two more weeks and you'll be coming home for good. We can hardly wait to have you home again.

Last week your dad was asked by the president of the college to apply for the position of vice-president. He told him no. He said he needed more time to be with his family. I talked to him about it and he said that having another title attached to his name wasn't that important to him anymore. To tell you the truth, I'm relieved. Your father has always been one who couldn't say no, and I think that sometimes people have taken advantage of that.

Tara and Craig seem to be spending a lot of time together, but every now and then he drops by to talk to us. Kim seems to have accepted the fact that she's mostly just going to be a friend to Craig. He told us the other day that he'd decided for sure to go on a mission, but that his parents are mad at him for wanting to use the money he's saved for college for a mission.

We have a new bishop in our ward. Bishop McDermott. I don't know if you remember him or not. He's very young to be a bishop. I doubt if he's even thirty yet. His wife's name is Nicole. She's a real beauty and a lot of fun to be with. They have two children and one on the way. I hope you have a chance to meet him. He seems to have a great love for the youth in the ward.

Kim is starting to come out of her shell a little more each day. That's good in a way. She has boys calling her all the time, just like you did at her age. That's the good news. The bad news is she's getting a little more spunky than before. If something's not just right, she lets us know about it. Actually I think it's quite healthy and I'm happy about it.

We think about you all the time and pray for your welfare.

Love,
Mom

Two days later she received a letter from Bishop McDermott:

Dear Stephanie,

Guess what, I'm your new bishop. If that's a surprise to you, imagine what it was to me!

I'd like for us to get better acquainted. You probably know my wife better than you do me. She was an adviser to the Mia Maid class before you left. She's a wonderful woman.

When you get back, I'd like to sit down and talk to you. My wife has told me how talented you are. She saw you several times at roadshow practice before you left. She says that when you walk up on stage, something magic happens.

I hope things are going well for you and that you'll come home soon.

Sincerely,
Bishop Alan McDermott

16

Stephanie flew home the first week in August. The whole family was at the airport to meet her.

As soon as she set her suitcases down in the living room, she began a discussion she'd carefully rehearsed with her counselor at the halfway house. "Mom and Dad and Kim, is it okay if we have family council now?"

"All right," David said.

"We can't have any more secrets between us, okay?"

"Okay."

"That means we have to talk about things that maybe you'd rather not talk about. Is that okay?"

"Yes." Emily glanced at David, then nodded in agreement.

"Okay. The first thing you need to know about me is that I'm still smoking cigarettes. So I need to know where I can smoke."

"Do you have to smoke in the house?" Kim complained. "I don't want my clothes smelling bad. How about the garage?"

"No way. I'd freeze out there in the winter. What about my room? I could smoke in the bathroom and have the fan on."

"You mean like you did when you were smoking pot?" Kim asked.

There was a long, awkward silence.

"Actually, Stephanie, we've made some changes," Emily said. "We've had Kim move into your room. You can have her room and use the bathroom at the end of the hall."

"Why'd you do that?"

"We did it just after you left. We felt it would be . . . safer . . . if you didn't have a room with its own bathroom . . . because of what happened."

"So you just booted me out of my room?"

"We did it just after you left when we were so mad about you using pot in this house."

"So I'm out of a room?"

"You have Kim's old room."

"I'm not ever going to use pot again."

"We just think it's better this way."

Stephanie sighed. "Well, all right, I guess I deserve that, but it still doesn't solve where I can smoke."

David came over and in a gesture of affection put both hands on Stephanie's shoulders. "We've been in this house fourteen years. When we first moved in, I dedicated this home to be a place of safety and peace for us all. I just can't allow you to smoke here. Is there some other way we can help provide for your needs?"

"Is it okay if I smoke in the backyard or in the car?"

"That's all right with me," David said. "Does anyone else object to that?"

Nobody did, and so that's what was decided on.

Stephanie unpacked in her new room, put some clothes in the hamper, went down to the kitchen and made a sandwich, turned on the TV, flipped through the channels, turned it off, and then announced, "I'll be back in time for supper."

David and Emily and Kim stared at her, but they tried

to be nonchalant. "Oh? Where are you going?" Emily asked.

"I don't know. Just out."

"Would you like Kim to go with you?"

"No, I just want to be alone for a while." She caught their stares. "Hey, don't look at me that way, okay? It's not like before. I'll be back about six."

They watched her drive away, wondering if they'd ever see her sober again.

The strain of having Stephanie home was too much for Emily. "I've got to lie down," she moaned. "I've got such a headache." She left them.

At six o'clock the table was set and the food was on the table, thanks mainly to David. Kim was on the phone and Emily was still resting. David went into their bedroom. He thought he would find Emily taking a nap, but her eyes were wide open. "Supper is ready," he said softly.

"Is Stephanie back yet?"

"No, not yet."

"I wonder if she'll come home drunk."

"I don't know."

"It's supposed to be over, but it never will be, will it," she said.

"Probably not. We'll always be worrying about our kids. It goes with the territory. Let's eat."

"I'm not hungry."

"Me neither, but we have to eat."

"Why do we?"

"For Kim."

Emily got out of bed.

"I didn't know what to do about gravy," he said. "I've never made it before."

"It'll be fine without."

"I suppose. I'll go tell Kim it's ready."

"Do you ever wish you hadn't married me?" Emily asked as he started out of the room.

He stopped. "Of course not. Why would you even ask a question like that?"

"Because I'm the one responsible for what's happened to Stephanie."

"How can you say that?"

"My natural father was an alcoholic. They say it's passed on. I must have passed it on to Stephanie."

"That's not true."

"What if it is?"

"Why is this coming up now when Stephanie's getting better?"

"Before this I had to be strong. But I can't be anymore. Oh, David, I feel so guilty everytime I see Stephanie, wondering if it was my fault."

"How can it be your fault? Did you force Stephanie to have that first drink?"

"No."

"Then it's not your fault. Look, we did the best we could in raising Stephanie. Oh sure, we made mistakes, but even if we'd done everything right, she still has her free agency. She has the right to make mistakes, and none of us can or should take that away from her. Besides, I think some good can come from this, both for her and for us. I've learned more about myself in the past three months than ever before. Maybe that's what counts — that we grow from life's experiences, whatever they are. There's one thing I'm certain about — if God knew any better way for us to progress in this life, he'd be using it. Maybe all that's important is that we do the best we can and depend on him to sort it all out later."

He asked if she'd like a priesthood blessing. She said yes. They were both in tears as he gave it, but it brought comfort to them both.

After that, Emily's agony went away for a while. But it never totally left her. Whenever she became tired or depressed, it returned again. She had to learn to live with it.

It was a quiet supper, each silently picking at portions of what was on their plates, waiting for Stephanie, wondering what shape she'd be in when they saw her again.

At six thirty they heard the car pull in and a door slam. Stephanie bounded into the room. "Hi, guys! Sorry I'm late. I went to AA and met some people and we were sitting around talking and I completely forgot about the time." She sat down at the table and heartily dug into the food. "I feel great!" she said with a big smile.

After supper Bishop McDermott and his wife, Nicole, came over to welcome Stephanie home. Stephanie liked him right away because of his sense of humor.

"Tell me the truth," he said. "Did you know who I was when you got my letter?"

"Well, not very well. I guess I didn't really know you before you were called to be a bishop."

"That's because of my pickup truck. I learned an important lesson. If you're ever in an elders quorum presidency, don't ever own a pickup truck. It seemed like all I did was help people move. When I finally figured out what was happening, I sold the truck and nobody ever asked me to help 'em move again."

His wife added, "And that's when they called him to be bishop."

He laughed. "Gosh, that's right, isn't it. Maybe I should have kept the pickup." He turned to Stephanie. "Just kidding."

"I don't think Stephanie knows what to make of you," Nicole said.

"Maybe you should tell her," he said.

"He's a wonderful bishop. The best thing about him is he loves youth. He's spent a lot of time getting to know each of the kids in our ward."

"Tell me about Tara," Stephanie said.

"Why do you want to know?" the bishop asked.

"Because of Craig. He's going with her, and, well, I sort of got him interested in the Church."

"Are you friends with Tara too?" the bishop asked.

"Not really. I never felt very comfortable with her. She's the kind of girl who goes around saying, 'I know I'm not perfect,' but nobody believes her."

Bishop McDermott smiled. "My wife's been telling me what an interesting person you are. She was right. We've got to go now, but sometime soon I'd like to talk with you in my office. Is that all right with you?"

"I guess so."

"Great. I'll have my executive secretary set up an appointment with you."

They left. Stephanie was impressed that they'd taken the time to come visit her.

The next day Craig came over right after work. He was still dressed in his work clothes, faded, sawdust-covered jeans and a T-shirt.

"I was wondering if you'd like to go canoeing up on Pactola."

"When?"

"Right now. I've got the canoe on my car."

"Okay. I'll need to change though."

"I'll wait."

It was awkward sitting beside him on their drive up to the lake. She wanted to be physically close to him, leaning against him, or at least holding hands, but he seemed far away and detached. She knew it was because of Tara.

When they got to the lake, they untied the canoe and set it in the water. He taught her a few things about paddling a canoe, and then they headed out, following the shoreline. Half an hour later they beached the canoe, climbed a hill, and sat and watched the sunset across the water.

Craig remained polite and yet somehow distant. For Stephanie, it was like talking to a cousin. She wanted him to hold her in his arms, but he didn't. As darkness set in, they paddled back to where they'd left the car.

On the way home, she sat close to him. "Why did you ask me to go with you tonight?" she asked.

"To welcome you back."

"I thought it might have been some sort of church assignment or something."

"Why would you think that?"

"Remember the first time we met? That's what I was hoping tonight would be like."

"We'd both been drinking that night."

"It wasn't the drinking, and you know it. It was us together. I want it to be like that again between us."

He paused. "I'm not sure that it ever can be like that again."

"Why not?"

"I have to be careful."

"What do you mean?"

"I've decided to go on a mission."

"So?"

"I just have to be careful, that's all. Tara's shown me there's other things besides physical attraction."

"What's wrong with physical attraction?"

"Nothing, I guess, except it can lead to trouble. Tara and I read the scriptures together every week. She came with me when I got my patriarchal blessing. She keeps me on the right track."

"Is she still going to BYU this fall?"

"Yes."

"Are you going there with her?"

"No, I need to save money for my mission."

At least that was good news. Tara would be gone and Craig would still be in town. "Do you wish I was more like Tara?"

He paused. "Sometimes."

"In what way?"

He sighed. "I can always count on Tara to live the right way."

It was a blow that both hurt and infuriated her. "I'm not good enough for you now, right?"

"No, that's not it."

"What is it then? Do you think I'll corrupt you?"

"Not really, but I just have to be careful."

"This isn't fair, Craig. I really think this whole thing stinks."

"Try and understand. Getting ready for a mission is the most important thing in my life right now."

"I'm not stopping you, am I?"

"No. It's just that I feel . . . safer with Tara than I do with you."

What she did next was done out of anger, and she regretted it almost as soon as it was done. "You don't mind if I smoke, do you?" She didn't wait for an answer. She pulled out a cigarette and lit up.

He glanced over and frowned. "That really disappoints me."

"Join the club." She blew smoke in his face. "That makes two of us disappointed tonight."

As soon as the car stopped, she opened the door and ran across the lawn, into the house, and up to her room.

Stephanie gave up on Craig, but also to some extent the Church too. Whenever the bishop's executive secretary called to try and set up an appointment with Bishop McDermott, she said she was too busy. She didn't care if she ever met with him.

Within a few days she found a whole new set of friends

among those her age involved in AA. They had, for the most part, also been through a rehab program. They were a strange group. Chad, his head shaved except for a strip of hair down the middle, usually showed up wearing a leather jacket and no shirt. Ryan, a street fighter, bragged that instead of getting mad, he got even. And the girls in AA were as tough and street-smart as the guys. Liz was a natural leader. She had long dark hair and wore black T-shirts, 501's, and hi-tops. She was now as dead set *against* alcohol and drugs as she had previously been *for* them.

Stephanie met once a day with the teen AA group and twice a day with the adult AA members. Before long she was asked to conduct some of the teen meetings. She and Liz and Chad alternated, leading the group in reading chapters from the AA book out loud and then responding to questions.

Before long Stephanie and Liz became best friends. Liz's situation at home was not good. Her parents were divorced, and her mother worked nights as a baker at a doughnut shop. Liz was seventeen and had a twelve-year-old sister and a nine-year-old brother that she had to take care of nights when her mother was working. It kept her at home a lot.

Stephanie brought Liz home a couple of times. David and Emily tried to find nice things to say about her, but it was hard to do, partly because Liz spoke street language. Emily cringed everytime Liz swore.

"I want to have a party and invite all my friends from Teen AA," Stephanie said one night to her mother.

"Oh, Stephanie, do you think that's a good idea?"

"Yeah, sure, why not?"

"I don't know. Just give me a little more time to adjust to them, okay?"

"Mom, there's nothing wrong with these people. Oh, sure, they look a little scary, but underneath it all, they're okay."

"I'm sure that's true, but . . . "

Stephanie should have pursued it further but she didn't. She kept her feelings inside of herself and let them smolder.

17

"I'm going to spend the night over at Liz's," Stephanie said a few days later.

"Will her parents be there?" Emily asked.

"No. There's only her mom, and she works nights."

"I don't feel good about you two girls being there without her mother. Will there be any boys?"

She hesitated. "Yes. Chad and Ryan."

"All night?"

"Yeah, so?"

"Then we'll have to say no," David said.

"Why?"

"Stephanie, you know why."

"Nothing's going to happen. We're just friends."

"You can stay there until midnight, and then I'll come and pick you up. We won't have you spending the night with boys."

Stephanie stormed out of the room. Two hours later she came down the stairs carrying a backpack. She walked up to her father, handed him a letter, and then turned to leave.

"Where are you going?" David asked.

"It's all in the letter. Goodbye." She walked out of the house and drove off.

David picked up the letter and began to read.

Dear Mom and Dad,

I have finally figured out a way to help you live a normal life with your perfect little family, which doesn't include me. I will NEVER be perfect or even close to it like you want me to be, no matter how hard I try, and believe me I really have been trying.

I know I've messed up the family for you by the way I used to live. I'm trying so hard to forget about that miserable life I had. But no matter what I do, it doesn't seem to really matter to either one of you. I know if I just leave you alone, it will make everything so much better. I have a few places I can stay where people will accept me for who I am. I know it's hard for you two to accept my past, especially with the way you were raised. You wanted me to turn out the way you are, but I didn't, so let's just face it and get on with our lives.

I have 46 days drug-free today. I don't know if that means anything to you but it's everything to me. I'm living my whole life right now to stay away from drugs.

I don't turn to drugs or alcohol when I have a problem anymore, so I know I can take care of myself. So don't worry. I know you will because you always think I'm going to mess up. Sometimes that really gets me down, knowing that my parents don't have faith in me.

If you only knew how good I'm doing. At least it seems to me I'm doing good compared to the past. I have good friends who care about me. I think I'm even helping people like me who are just starting in AA.

When I feel like I'm doing so good and feel mature enough to make the right decisions, then I ask you a simple question. I wouldn't have even asked to stay the night with Liz if I didn't think it was a good idea. The only way I'm ever going to be able to live a happy life and continue my plan of staying drug-free is to move out. I know I can do it, and I hope you believe in me too. Tomorrow I'm going to talk to Liz's mother. I know I can stay there. I know you'd rather I stay here but the only way I can live here and be a happy person is if I have a lot more freedom. I'll talk to you tomorrow before I go to stay with Liz for good. I'm just too grown up right now to be treated like a little kid. I just want to get out and live my own life.

Whenever I bring my friends from AA home, you both act like you're being attacked by a street gang. These are my friends now, and if they're not good enough for you, then maybe I'm not good enough for you either.

You don't know how hard I'm trying to stay clean and all the sacrifices I've made. Even the friends like Jessica I've lost. But the friends I've met recently, like Liz and Chad and Ryan, really care about me. It feels real good to have them around me. They help me so much. Especially Liz. This world is real scary alone, but I got people around me, so don't worry.

I love you both very much even though you are so hard to figure out. I'll see you in the morning when I come to pick up all my stuff. Goodbye.

Stephanie

"What are we going to do?" Emily asked after reading the letter.

"I don't even know where Liz lives. Do you?"

"No."

"Then I guess we can't do anything tonight. She says she'll be back tomorrow to pick up her things." He paused. "For starters, let's each write her a letter."

This was David's letter to Stephanie:

Dear Stephanie,

Thanks for your beautiful letter. You're really

grown up to be able to communicate your feelings in such a clear way.

I'm glad you're in this family. You make me stop and think instead of just acting like I used to do.

I'm proud of you for having 46 days of sobriety. Congratulations!

I'm surprised you think it is hard for us to accept your past. We are trying to show we accept your past and love you for how you are now. I'm sorry you think we are worried about you messing up when we give you a restriction or a guideline or a rule or a list or a precaution. You get upset because you think that means we don't trust you. We have a far different reason for saying these things. I'm glad you raised the issue so I can explain.

The path to freedom is based on people agreeing to certain principles and even setting some guidelines so they know how to get along. These are sometimes made-up rules or lists, but they result in more freedom. Freedom requires rules.

If you have your friends in this house, they must understand there are rules. The first is that we don't want them smoking in our house. The second is that we don't want R- or X-rated movies shown. The third rule is that if they stay overnight, the boys have to sleep in one room and the girls in another.

You may not think it's fair for me to impose rules on your friends. Maybe it isn't, but you have to realize that I'm the one who makes the house payment, and I figure I ought to have a few rights about what happens in my house.

One thing I regret is that I haven't done anything to show your friends from AA that I appreciate the support they're giving you to stay off drugs and alcohol. So I'm not without fault in this. I'm willing to make changes in my life if you're willing to do the same.

Whatever you do, don't go live under somebody else's rules. Stay here and help us learn together. You'll be graduating before long, and then you'll probably be leaving home. We all have such a short time left together.

Love,
Dad

This was Emily's letter, which she wrote very early the next morning:

Dear Stephanie,

I stayed awake many hours last night worrying about you and wondering what to do.

I love you very much. As Dad says, you help us learn. That's kind of strange that parents have to learn too, isn't it? When I was young I thought parents knew everything. Little did I know about their struggles and worries for me as a child. Of course, you only realize this after you're a parent yourself. Sometimes it's tough being a parent.

Please don't give up on us. Let's get together and talk often or do something together. We need you here in our family. You are such an important link in our eternal family circle. Come back and live with us.

I admit being a little nervous about your new friends. You'll have to admit they're not like any of the people at church, but we respect your judgment. If you feel good about them, then they're welcome in this home, as long as they're willing to abide by the rules Dad told you about in his letter.

That was a beautiful letter you wrote us, and it showed a lot of thought on your part. Your dad and I were very impressed.

We love you, Stephanie.

Mom.

The next day about eleven thirty Stephanie showed up. "Hi. I'll just be a few minutes packing up my things, and then I'll get out of here. I'll leave the car here. Liz is outside waiting for me in her car."

"Dad and I each wrote you a letter," Emily said. "They're on your dresser. Will you read them before you start packing?"

"Okay." She went up to her room.

Emily sat down at the kitchen table, bowed her head, and prayed.

Minutes later Stephanie came down. Her eyes were red.

"Will you stay with us?" Emily asked.

"Yes."

Emily threw her arms around Stephanie and told her again and again how much she loved her.

For the third time that night Stephanie drove around the block where Jessica lived. More than anything she wanted to stop and go in. She missed the fun they'd had together.

Jessica had phoned a couple of times while Stephanie was out, but Stephanie had never returned the call. Actually she dreaded seeing her again, not knowing for sure if she was strong enough to turn down Jessica's invitation to party. Right now it was all she could do to stay sober. That's why she attended three AA meetings a day.

Nobody knew how hard it was for her. She was sure her parents thought that since she'd been through treatment, the problem was solved. But it wasn't. Each day was a new challenge.

Stephanie pulled over and parked in front of Jessica's house. *I'll just go in for a minute,* she thought. *It'll be okay. We'll just talk. No, I can't do that. She'll want me to have just one drink but I can't stop with one. I've got to be strong or else everything will start in all over again.*

She started the car and drove home, grateful to have stayed sober one more day.

More than anything, she dreaded seeing Jessica again.

*　　　*　　　*　　　*　　　*

Stephanie went to church on Sunday with her family, more for their sake than for anything else. She left after sacrament meeting because she didn't feel a part of the Church anymore. Also, she couldn't stand to see Tara and Craig together.

Right after her parents got home from church, Bishop McDermott came over to see Stephanie.

"My executive secretary tells me he's having a tough time getting an appointment set up for you and me," he said.

"Yeah, well, I *have* been giving him the run-around."

"Why?"

"I don't see any reason for me to talk to you. I mean, let's face it, there's no place for me in this church."

"Why do you say that?"

"I've messed up too many times."

"There's no 'too many times' for the Savior. Look, let's get together at least once and talk."

"We're talking now."

"I mean in my office. Have you had lunch yet?"

"No."

"Me either. How about if you meet me at the church at two thirty?"

"It'll just be a waste of time for you."

He smiled. "Not really. It'll get me out of doing dishes."

"All right, but don't expect much."

Bishop McDermott closed the door. "I appreciate your coming in," he said as he sat down at his desk.

"Bishop, don't ask me questions you really don't want to know the answer to—I don't lie anymore, and I won't for you either, even if it means you end up kicking me out of the Church. I'm an alcoholic and a drug addict. I'm still a virgin, although it's been close a couple of times. Most of my friends are in AA. I prefer them over members of the Church actually because they accept me for what I am and they help me stay sober. Oh yeah, I smoke cigarettes and swear a lot. And you can forget about asking me to go to the Laurel class anymore. Is there anything else you'd like to know about me?"

"Do you think much about God?"

"Hey, I'm doing great in that department these days, but I don't really expect you to believe that."

"Why wouldn't I believe it?"

"Because you probably think God is just for Mormons. That's not true, you know. God helps all kinds of people — even people you wouldn't want to be seen with. Like my friends in AA. One of the first things they teach in AA is you need to place your life in God's hands and let him take charge. After each AA meeting we hold hands and have a prayer. And God hears us. I've gone almost two months alcohol- and drug-free with God's help. So it must work, right?"

"It works for you, and that's great. Congratulations."

"Thanks. One thing you've got to realize — I don't need the Church the way some girls do. I can get along okay without it."

"That's because AA is like a church, isn't it?"

"Yeah, I guess it is."

"I'm familiar with the twelve steps of AA," he said. "To me it's like twelve steps of repentance. I believe God inspired the people who started AA."

She smiled. "Hey, what's going on here? You're agreeing with me too much. It must mean you're planning to soften me up so you can ask me to do something. What is it?"

"We need you, Stephanie."

"Why? You want me to give a fireside on drugs and scare little kids to death? Sure, I'll tell 'em if they don't watch out, they'll end up like me. That ought to keep 'em on the straight and narrow, right?"

The bishop reached over for his scriptures and laid them on the desk in front of him.

"Look, Bishop, you got to understand one thing. It'll never be like it was before I started messing up."

"I know that, but, on the other hand, because of your experiences, there are people in this ward you can help that nobody else can reach. We need you to be a part of us again."

"You'd better talk to Craig about me. He'll tell you I'm no good. That's why he broke up with me. He was afraid I'd corrupt him or something."

"Would you have?"

"No, I don't think so. I know one thing though—I'm not going to get active in the Church just for him. If he doesn't like me the way I am, well then he can forget it. I'm not changing for him."

"You're right, you shouldn't change for him. Do it for yourself, because it'll make you happier."

"I'm plenty happy the way I am. Besides, there's nobody in the Church, except maybe you, who really cares about me."

"This is the Savior's church, and he loves you. And God loves you."

"God loves me in AA. I'm not so sure he does in this church."

"He does here too. I'm sure of it."

Stephanie was certain the bishop meant it.

"There's one more thing I need to say about AA," he said. "I'm not sure you're ready for it now, but if you're not, just store it somewhere in your mind until you are. Okay?"

"Okay."

"In my own family I've seen what good AA can do for people. My uncle is an alcoholic. Ten years ago, after losing his job and nearly his family, he finally turned to AA. It turned his entire life around. So I know what a good job they do. I want you spend as much time there as you need to. I'm sure you'll be able to help others there too. But there's one thing you need to know: as wonderful as it is, it can't bring you all of the Lord's blessings, because it's not the restored gospel of Jesus Christ. They have no priesthood power and they don't have the saving ordinances. That may not mean very much to you now, but someday it will. We want you here with us. We want you to think about the possibility of someday entering the temple of the Lord and being sealed to a worthy young man for time and eternity."

"Bishop, I still don't think you understand. I've done some real bad things in my life."

"It doesn't matter—God never gives up on anybody. Look, maybe we should talk about repentance." Using the scriptures, he went through the steps of repentance with her.

After he finished, she said, "By confession, you mean you want me to tell you the bad things I've done?"

"Yes."

She shook her head. "I'm not ready for that yet."

"All right."

"Can we talk about something else for a while?" she asked.

"Sure, what would you like to talk about?"

"Tara."

"What about her?"

"You interview her too, don't you?"

"Yes. I interviewed her a few weeks ago."

"Is she as good as she lets on to be?"

"Yes."

"That is *so* depressing."

"Why?"

"Because with girls like her around, I don't have a chance."

"What is it about her that you most admire?"

189

"Hey, I didn't say I admired her. Craig's the one who does that."

"All right, what is it about her that Craig admires?"

"Beats me."

He grinned. "Is this a jealous female I'm hearing?"

"She's like, 'Oh, gosh, this is the first day of the rest of our lives. Isn't that special?' "

The bishop tried not to laugh but didn't succeed.

"You know what, Bishop? I bet she's never had a zit in her whole life. And then there's me. I used to buy Clearasil in five-gallon drums. I'm serious."

Bishop McDermott laughed.

"Tara always looks so . . . "—she searched for the word—" . . . lovely. Yes, that's it, she's lovely. Her lovely hair, her lovely smile . . . If you want to know the truth, she makes me sick."

"Why? You're just as beautiful as she is."

"If it were just the way we looked, I'd come out okay. But it isn't. Tara's got it made in other areas."

"Like what?"

She paused. "She never took that first drink."

"You wish you hadn't done that now, don't you?"

"Oh yeah, in the worst way. See, the thing is that I'm an alcoholic now, and I'll be one for the rest of my life. I'll always be one drink away from hell. But that's not all either. The alcohol also got me into pot and a bunch of other drugs and, right at the last, cocaine. For the rest of my life I'll have this gun pointing at my head. Will I ever start up again? That's the one thing that scares me to death just thinking about." She sighed. "Actually, if you want to know the truth, I don't blame Craig for switching to Tara. If I were him, I would've done it too."

"Would it surprise you to know Tara has things she's working on?"

"I don't believe it."

"Not major things, but still, things about her she'd like

to improve. As far as that goes, I do too. You know, if you'd start going to Young Women, it might help you. They have goals they work on."

"The only goal I've got right now is to stay sober. That's it. After that, to finish high school. I'm not sure about college. I'm afraid if I ever get stressed out, I might start drinking again."

"Try going to Young Women next week."

"It won't work. Nobody in this church wants me the way I am now."

"Why not?"

She shook her head. "Look, the truth is, my mind is a cesspool. It's not just the alcohol or the drugs. It's a whole lot more than that. It's all the raunchy movies I've seen at parties. It's watching guys trying to get girls drunk so they can go to bed with them. It's all the swear words and all the dirty jokes I've been exposed to. It's being so good at telling lies that sometimes I can't tell what the truth is. It's all the times I set people up to get hurt when we were playing Quarters." She looked at him. "You don't even know about playing Quarters, do you?"

"No."

"You put a cup on the floor in the corner and then everybody tries to toss a quarter into it. If you do it, then you get to choose who has to take the next drink. Sounds harmless, right? Except that everybody decides beforehand who they're out to get that night. So we all choose the same guy, or sometimes it's a girl we're out to get. So we purposely get somebody disgustingly drunk. Sometimes we were like a pack of mean dogs. One time we got this airhead girl drunk and the next day I found out some guys had taken advantage of her in the back seat of a car after she'd passed out. The thing is, I didn't even care." She paused. "How could I not have cared? Why didn't I stop her from getting so drunk? That's what I mean, Bishop."

191

She tapped her forehead. "It's all in here, all the things I'm so ashamed of now."

"You're not the first person in the world who's made serious mistakes." He wrote down something on a piece of paper and handed it to her. "Read this for next time."

She looked at what he'd written, *Mosiah, chapter 27*. "Is there going to be a next time?" she asked.

"Yes, if you'll agree to it."

"Why are you wasting your time with me?"

"You have a lot of secrets about yourself, but I know the most important secret of all about you."

"What?"

He smiled. "We'll talk about it next time. Meanwhile you make sure and read that chapter in Mosiah."

That night she read: "Nevertheless, after wading through much tribulation, repenting nigh unto death, the Lord in mercy hath seen fit to snatch me out of an everlasting burning, and I am born of God. My soul hath been redeemed from the gall of bitterness and bonds of iniquity. I was in the darkest abyss; but now I behold the marvelous light of God. My soul was racked with eternal torment; but I am snatched, and my soul is pained no more."

"How are you getting along these days?" Bishop McDermott asked the next time they met in his office.

"I feel worse now than before I started meeting with you."

"I hope it's not something I've said."

"It's not you. When I was using all the time I never felt guilty. It was like whatever I did was okay. But now I remember things I didn't think were bad at the time, but now I know they were. So I keep feeling worse as time goes on. When is it going to get better?"

"What might be happening is that you're getting closer to the Savior. As we do that, we all begin to see ourselves in a new light, how good he is compared to us. We are all so dependent on him. Things we thought weren't that bad we now see in a new light. We become more aware of our own weaknesses and at the same time more grateful to the Savior for making it possible for us to be forgiven."

"Bishop, do you really still think I can be forgiven?"

"I'm sure of it."

"When will I know I've been forgiven?"

"Did you read the passage in Mosiah I gave you last time?"

"Yes."

"You'll know the same way Alma knew." He read again from the writings of Alma in chapter 27 of Mosiah: " 'I was in the darkest abyss; but now I behold the marvelous light of God. My soul was racked with eternal torment; but I am snatched, and my soul is pained no more.' "

"I want that to happen to me."

"It will come in time."

"I forgot to tell you something last time. Remember that girl I was telling you about last time? The one we played Quarters with? Well, there's one thing I haven't told you yet. She got pregnant and had an abortion. The thing is, some of my quarters I tossed into that cup helped get her drunk and that led to other things. Sometimes I get to feeling so bad."

"Maybe you should ask your father for a priesthood blessing."

Stephanie remembered back to the last time she'd had a father's blessing.

She began to cry.

The next night Stephanie opened the door to her father's office and watched him working at his desk. She noticed he was starting to show his age, and he looked tired.

In all the group sessions she'd attended, she had heard many stories of fathers who had abused or abandoned their kids, and yet there was her own dad, constant and dependable through whatever happened.

He noticed her at the door. "Do you need anything?" he asked.

"The bishop asked me to see if you'd give me a priesthood blessing." She paused. "I sort of feel guilty asking you though."

"Why?"

"Because when you gave me one before, I didn't even try to quit using. I really feel bad about that now. I'm sorry for all the grief I've caused you and Mom. I love you, Daddy."

He stood up. "I love you too, more than you'll ever know. Let's see about that priesthood blessing now."

She sat in the chair and felt her father's gentle hands on her head as he blessed her. Afterwards, as they hugged each other, they both felt a little foolish because their tears wouldn't stop.

The blessing worked. She felt a comforting influence, which stayed with her for a long time.

18

"Mom, I want to have a party with my friends from AA," Stephanie said a couple of days later.

Her mother cleared her throat. "Well, okay."

"You're still not too crazy about the idea, are you."

Her mother smiled faintly. "Not really."

"Come to AA with me then and that'll help you get better acquainted."

Emily tried to be brave. "I'll go if that's what you want me to do."

Stephanie started to laugh.

"What's wrong?" Emily asked.

"You look so scared."

The meeting was at an old warehouse on the edge of the tracks, a boxlike building with no windows. Inside, the hall was packed and smoke-filled. A meeting of AA bikers had just let out. Stephanie led her mother past bearded men in leather jackets. One reached out and tapped Emily on the shoulder. "Hey, Mama, what's happening?" Emily turned neither to the right nor to the left, following Stephanie to the room where the teenaged members of AA met once a day. There, tables were laid out into a square with chairs placed around them.

Each person had a booklet from AA, and they would

each take turns reading. After a few minutes they came to questions. One person would read the question and then answer it.

At first Emily felt as though she was attending a meeting of a street gang. The way the people dressed and their language bothered her. But as the meeting progressed, she heard them talk about how hard they were trying to make it through another day, and she began to respect them.

At the end of the meeting, they all stood in a circle and held hands and prayed. Liz said the prayer. She didn't use *thou* and *thee,* but what she said was from her heart. Emily opened her eyes and looked around. Suddenly it was as if she were seeing these kids in a new light, as if they were the royal sons and daughters of a king, people who, as a whim, dressed in the most bizarre outfits for a costume party. But underneath the outward appearance, they were all, like her own daughter, still children of the greatest King of all. She knew they had a tougher battle every day, just to stay sober, than she ever had when she was growing up.

On the way home, Emily said, "I feel much better about your friends now."

"Thanks, Mom. I knew you'd see the good in them like I do."

When they got home, Emily and Stephanie sat down and made plans for a party.

Emily had never made so many preparations for a party in her life. There was the food, of course. Stephanie asked for Domino's Pizza and diet soda. Emily offered to bake a cake, but Stephanie said no.

Then the house had to be prepared. Emily spent an hour cleaning the house and two hours hiding her jewelry and other precious belongings so they wouldn't be stolen. Better to be on the safe side, she thought to herself.

She didn't want to put temptation in the way of these

guests, so she hid her vanilla extract and her Nyquil and Tylenol in David's fishing gear in the garage.

The next thing to worry about was party games. She went to the library. "Do you have a book of party games?" she asked the librarian.

"For children or for adults?"

"Not exactly either. They're more like . . . juvenile delinquents."

The librarian gave her a strange look. "Juvenile delinquents don't play party games. They get drunk and knife each other."

"These kids won't be drinking, and I hope they won't be knifing each other either, because my daughter is one of them. Don't you have any idea of games they'd enjoy playing?"

The librarian shrugged her shoulders. "We don't get many requests like this. If you want, I can see about ordering a book on interlibrary loan."

"No, thanks. We'll work something out. The party's tomorrow night."

Emily finally asked Stephanie, and she suggested getting some movies at the video store.

"No R-rated movies," Emily said.

"I know."

Stephanie and her mother spent two hours at the video store. The problem was to find a movie acceptable to them both. Stephanie picked out a horror movie. Emily read the description of the movie and asked, "Why would anyone want to see this?"

"It's not that bad. There's like only four or five people who get chopped up with a chain saw. Mom, it's just a movie."

"All right, just turn it on low enough so I don't hear the screaming."

At six thirty on Saturday night Stephanie's friends began to show up. Emily and David met and talked with them until they drifted into the TV room.

At seven the pizzas showed up. Emily opened them and carried them into the family room, where everyone was sprawled on the floor watching the movie.

"Okay, now this one is sausage and this is Canadian bacon," Emily called out, as blood and gore filled the TV screen. It didn't seem to hurt anyone's appetite. She made a quick retreat back to the kitchen just as the chain saw started up again.

At seven thirty Stephanie came out of the room.

"What's wrong?" Emily asked.

"We turned off the movie."

"What for?"

"Everybody's seen it before. You got anything else we can do?"

"Get everybody together. I'll be in in a minute."

Emily tried to think back on years of being a mother. The first thing she said to the group was, "Has anyone ever played 'This is a cow, this is a horse'?"

Nobody had.

"Great. Have you ever played Chinese writing?"

They played games the rest of the night. As the party broke up, Chad, the boy with a Mohawk, told Stephanie, "Your mom is cool."

That made Emily's day.

Stephanie's next meeting with Bishop McDermott occurred the next day after church.

"Bishop, one time you said you knew the most important secret about me. What is it?"

"Can't you guess?"

She thought about it. "It's the old 'I'm a child of God' bit, right?"

"Right."

"I figured it was something like that."

"I can tell you're not impressed."

"I've been singing 'I Am a Child of God' ever since I was a little kid."

"Maybe you should start singing it again."

"Oh, sure."

"I'm serious. The one thing you need to be absolutely certain of is that God still loves you, that it's not too late for you to repent and be forgiven."

"You always keep coming back to that, don't you. Why?"

"It's the most important thing I can tell you right now."

Slowly she began to think that maybe the bishop was right about the things he kept saying to her.

"Have you ever met Craig's parents?" the bishop asked the next time they met.

"Yeah, sure. Why?"

"Did you get along with them okay?"

"Yeah, I like 'em both. Why do you ask?"

"They're having a tough time accepting the fact that Craig wants to go on a mission. Why don't you go talk to them sometime?"

"Why me? You're the bishop. You ought to be the one to do that."

"You give it a try first, okay?"

Two days later she stood at the Millers' door and knocked.

Craig's mother came to the door.

"I don't know if you remember me, but I'm Stephanie. I came here once . . . to change clothes."

"Craig's not here."

"I know. I came to talk to you and your husband."

"Come in."

They went in the living room. Mr. Miller was watching an exhibition football game.

"We've got company," Mrs. Miller said.

199

He looked over at her. "What do you want?"

"I just wanted to see how you both were doing."

Mrs. Miller turned off the TV. "How would you be doing if you'd lost your son?"

"What do you mean?"

"He has no use for us anymore. Everytime we turn around, he's running over to that church of his."

"Between his church and that girl of his, we never see him anymore," Mr. Miller said. "And now he tells us he's going to take all the money he's been saving for college to go be a missionary. He didn't even ask us what we thought about the idea."

"That must be hard on you," Stephanie said.

"It's like anything we tell him isn't important because we're not Mormons."

"He'll grow out of that." She paused. "The reason I came over was to invite you both and Craig over for supper on Thursday."

"Why?"

"I'd just like you to meet my parents. I've told them a lot about how good you were to me when I was going with Craig."

"And you won't try and convert us?"

"No, but we have invited two missionaries. But don't worry, they won't do much of anything except eat. I just want us all to get better acquainted, that's all."

On Thursday Stephanie worked in the kitchen all day. Following her mother's directions, she made rolls and baked a pie and a cake and put the roast in the oven and even prepared real mashed potatoes.

Craig's folks were at first very uncomfortable until David, coached beforehand by Stephanie, announced he was a Boston Celtic fan.

Craig's father kept looking over at the two missionaries, waiting for the sales pitch that never came. Finally his curiosity got the best of him. "Why are you two out here when you could be getting an education?"

That opened things up. After fifteen minutes of talking with the missionaries about what they did on their mission, Craig's mother said, "He could be doing a lot worse things with his life than this."

"What if he uses up all his money for a mission and never finishes college?" his dad said.

"You never finished college," his mother said. "And you turned out all right."

"I know, but Craig's different. He's got a real future ahead of him if he'll just get a good education."

"I promise I'll finish college after my mission," Craig said.

Nothing spectacular happened. And yet a few days later Craig's parents told Craig they wouldn't object if he went on a mission.

19

Because Stephanie was the big sister who knew what looked good, Kim started asking her for advice. They spent hours in the mall trying on clothes.

Stephanie hoped her bad example would not cause Kim to start drinking or using drugs. As time went on, though, she began to feel that Kim was going to turn out all right after all.

Kim was becoming more beautiful day by day. Sometimes Stephanie wondered if Kim and Craig would someday get married. Craig still came around to see Kim, and they talked a lot at church between meetings.

Craig and Stephanie became more friendly too. He was grateful for what she'd done to smooth things out with his parents. He called her once or twice a week, and they started to treat each other more as friends. A few times she even gave him advice when he had a problem with Tara.

Near the end of August Tara left for BYU. Craig, faithful and true, wrote three times a week.

When school started, Stephanie transferred to Central High School. She wanted to go where nobody, especially the teachers, knew her, where she could make a new start, and where she could avoid seeing Jessica and her friends.

One nice thing about being at Central was that Liz was there. They shared a locker and ate lunch together and went to AA meetings together after school.

School seemed harder to Stephanie than before. She found it harder to concentrate. Her father said it would come back to her, but she wondered if she had permanently messed up her mind with chemicals. She knew only time would tell.

Stephanie's biggest accomplishment in September was that she quit smoking. During the time when her craving for a cigarette was the worst, she began to feel as though she was single-handedly supporting the company that made Life Savers.

Near the end of September Bishop McDermott saw Stephanie in the hall at church and asked her to give a talk in sacrament meeting.

"Get out of here. You don't want me to talk in church."

"I do."

"What are you trying to do? Get released from being a bishop?"

"Heavenly Father wants you to talk in sacrament meeting."

"I don't know. I'm not that terrific at giving talks."

"Ask your dad for help then."

"You're really serious about this?"

"Absolutely."

"I'd like to thank the bishop for letting me do this. I bet he's a lot more nervous right now than I am." Stephanie turned around to Bishop McDermott and flashed him a teasing smile.

"I'm Stephanie and I'm an alcoholic and a drug addict. That's what we say in AA. It gets everything out in the open right away."

She talked about rebellious youth in the Old Testament,

and said that how no matter how righteous the parents were, sometimes their children made bad choices.

She closed her talk with this:

"If you want your kids to be like you, all you can do is set a good example. Maybe they'll follow that, and maybe they won't. But I think eventually they will. I know my mom and dad have always set a good example for me. Now I'm beginning to think I want to be more like them when I grow up.

"I've done a lot of things I'm not proud of. The bishop and I are working through it all. I know I've done wrong and I'm sorry. I've hurt a lot of people. I've hurt my parents most of all, and I've hurt Kim by not being a better example for her. I just want you all to know that I'm sorry and I'm trying to do better, but it's going to take a while—hey, maybe even my whole life.

"I want to say something to you kids out there, you ten- and eleven- and twelve-year-olds. I was twelve when I first started drinking. You can do the same as me if you want, but let me tell you something I found out: the only thing it'll bring you is grief. So, whatever you do, don't take that first drink or that first anything. And if you already have, give it up, if you can by yourself, and if you can't, get help. I have so many friends in AA. I'll take you there any time you want to go.

"I'm glad Jesus can help us change and that he never gives up on us. I don't know Jesus as well as I'd like to, so I'm glad I've got the bishop around to sort of fill me in until I get on my feet a little more. He talks a lot about Jesus. And he also keeps telling me I can make it in this church. I guess that's the main reason I'm still here.

"I love my mom and my dad and my sister. They've really stuck by me through everything. I know it hasn't been easy for them. I've disappointed them a lot of times, but they never gave up on me.

"I see Craig out there. I'm really glad he joined the

Church. I know he'll make a good missionary. In a way I'm glad he's been going with Tara, because she's so good. I really admire her, and I wish I was more like her. Maybe someday I will be.

"I'm glad that Liz and Chad and Ryan came to church today to hear me talk. I know they look kind of different, but really, once you get to know them, they're the best friends a person could ever have.

"I know there's a God and that he answers prayers. I couldn't get through a day without God's help. And that's the truth. In the name of Jesus Christ. Amen."

Craig called her after church and told her how much he enjoyed her talk. Then, after a long pause, he said, "Last week Tara wrote and said she thought we should start dating other people. She says she's met a returned missionary in her ward at BYU."

"Well, now."

"Are you snickering?" he asked.

"No, why?"

"You are snickering, Stephanie. Don't deny it."

"All right, maybe a small insignificant snicker escaped my lips, but then I stopped. I'm very good at stopping things, you know."

"So anyway, I've decided to start dating again." He paused. "I was wondering if you'd go with me to a young adult activity Saturday."

It was a perfect day for a church party. A warm October breeze caused a few yellow and brown leaves to fall to the ground like colored rain.

The fifteen young adults met at the ward at four o'clock and then drove to Custer State Park, where they began their hike to the top of Harney Peak.

Near the beginning of their hike, Craig reached for her

hand. She raised her eyebrows. "For safety," he said, "in case one of us falls."

"You can never be too safe, that's for sure," she teased.

They held hands and walked slowly. Soon everyone else had passed and gone ahead.

"We've always been friends," he said, "but lately, I don't know, it's better." He stopped and looked at her. "I'm glad you're trying to live right."

"I haven't changed for you," she said. "I did it for me."

"I know."

"The thing I'm finding out is that I haven't given up anything really important."

After they'd hiked for a while, she was too warm. She took off her sweater and tied it around her waist. She glanced up and saw him staring at her. "What?"

"Nothing. I just like to look at you." He paused. "I wrote Tara last night."

"Oh."

"I told her I agree with her that we ought to date other people. I want to spend a lot of time with you until I leave on my mission." He looked down, then directly at her. "Stephanie, I think I'm in love with you."

She felt as if she had always loved him, but she wasn't sure if she should tell him or not. She didn't want him feeling boxed-in on his mission by her expectations of marriage. She longed for the time when she could tell him everything and could show him how much she loved him. But this wasn't that time. That would have to wait until they were married. "I love you too, Craig."

He kissed her.

"Well," she said after they broke apart. "We'd better start up again, or they'll think something happened to us."

He laughed. "Something did happen to us."

"Yes, I know. Something very nice."

"I hope you're still around when I get back from my mission."

"I hope so too."

They started walking again. As they rounded a turn, the end of the trail was in sight. She punched him on the shoulder. "Race you to the top," she said, taking off.

When they got to the top, they sat down to catch their breath and to gaze at the magnificent view around them.

Not long after that, it was time to start down. Because some of the others had teased Craig and Stephanie for taking so long on the way up, they decided to be the first ones down the trail.

"I'm dying of thirst," she said as they jogged down.

"There's watermelons when we get to the bottom. I picked 'em out. I don't know if you know it or not, but I'm an expert in knowing how to pick a good watermelon."

"What's your secret?"

"You tap it, right? Well, if it taps back, whatever you do, don't pick that one."

She started laughing. The sound seemed to carry for miles.

It was, ironically enough, on the same day that Stephanie received her patriarchal blessing—the day she was reminded that before her birth she had been loved and cherished by God, the day she felt a sense of her own nobility in being a daughter of Father in heaven, the day the Spirit testified to her that God loved her still and that it wasn't too late for her to inherit the blessings of eternity, the day she felt forgiven of past mistakes—that she finally confronted Jessica.

Stephanie and her family had traveled to Belle Fourche, where the stake patriarch lived. She and Kim both received their blessings that day. After it was over, they threw their arms around each other and wept tears of joy.

On the way home they passed the mall. Stephanie asked her father if they could stop because she needed to get some shampoo. Everyone else was too tired to go in, so Stephanie went in by herself while the family waited in the car.

She bought the shampoo in the drugstore and was on her way out when she spotted Jessica. She tried to pass by unnoticed, hoping that she hadn't been seen.

"Hey, woman, where you been keeping yourself?" Jessica called out.

Stephanie stopped. Jessica, in tank top and jeans, stumbled over to her. She looked terrible and smelled of stale beer. Two guys and a girl were with her. They weren't in any better shape than Jessica.

"What are you doing tonight?" Jessica asked. "There's a party at my house. My mom is gone for the weekend, so we'll be going all night. You'll come, won't you?"

"No, I guess not. Thanks anyway."

"Hey, I insist. It's your welcome-home party. C'mon, we'll have sooo much fun, just like before you left."

"I don't do that anymore."

"C'mon, you can't fool me with that 'I've become a new person' routine. C'mon, maybe we'll play Quarters. You remember Quarters, don't you?"

"Look, I really have to go. My parents are waiting in the car. I just came in for some shampoo. I'll see you later."

As she started to leave, Jessica grabbed her arm and turned her around. "Hey, what's the deal here? You think you're too good to party with your friends?"

Stephanie tried to get away, but Jessica wouldn't let go.

"Answer my question, will you? Do you think you're too good to have a couple of beers with us?"

There was, for Stephanie now, only one answer to that question. "Yes, Jessica, I am too good for that."

The two girls stared at each other.

"When you're ready to quit, let me know. Goodbye, Jessica."

Stephanie returned to her family waiting in the car.

What a Parent Can Do
If a Child Is Using Drugs or Alcohol

1. *Become informed.* Several helpful books may be found at the public library and at Alcoholics Anonymous. The following books were useful in researching background for *Stephanie:*
   a. Lewis B. Hancock, *When Drugs Hit Home* (Salt Lake City: Deseret Book, 1987).
   b. Toby Rice Drews, *Getting Your Children Sober* (South Plainfield, NJ: Bridge Publishing Company, 1987).
   c. Bob Meehan, *Beyond the Yellow Brick Road* (Chicago: Contemporary Books, 1984).
   d. *How to Keep the Children You Love Off Drugs* (New York: Atlantic Monthly Press, 1988).
   e. *Kids, Drugs, and Alcohol* (White Hall, VA: Betterway Publications, Inc., 1987).
   f. Robert L. DuPont, Jr., M.D., *Getting Tough on Gateway Drugs* (Washington, DC: American Psychiatric Press, Inc., 1984).
2. *Assure your son or daughter of your love.* Hugs need to go along with appropriate discipline.
3. *Determine what treatment options exist in your local area.*
   a. Call mental health agencies, hospitals, and private facilities and ask what is available.
   b. Look in the white pages of your telephone book for Alcoholics Anonymous. Ask if there is a teen AA group. Ask also about a support group for the rest of the family.
   c. Look in the yellow pages of your telephone book under Alcoholism Treatment and also Drug Abuse Information and Treatment. Call the organizations listed and ask for recommendations. Facilities in other communities can be found by looking in out-of-town telephone directories at the public library.
   d. Determine where the nearest in-patient facilities for treating chemical dependency are located. Are they strictly for youth, or are people of all ages treated?
   e. Contact LDS Social Services and ask for recommendations.
   f. Meet with your bishop and discuss treatment options with him.
   g. Find a support group and begin meeting with it. Ask parents who have already been through treatment with their youth for suggestions on what to do.
4. *Pray for inspiration and guidance. Then make an informed, reasoned decision and act on it.*

WHAT TO DO IF YOU NEED HELP

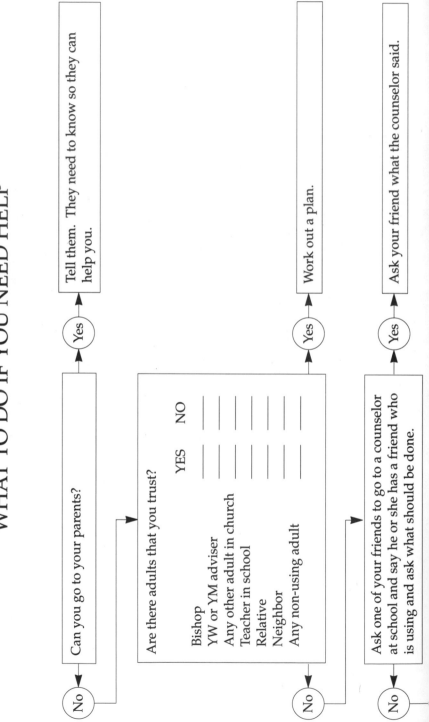

Can you go to your parents?

Yes → Tell them. They need to know so they can help you.

No →

Are there adults that you trust?

	YES	NO
Bishop	____	____
YW or YM adviser	____	____
Any other adult in church	____	____
Teacher in school	____	____
Relative	____	____
Neighbor	____	____
Any non-using adult	____	____

Yes → Work out a plan.

No →

Ask one of your friends to go to a counselor at school and say he or she has a friend who is using and ask what should be done.

Yes → Ask your friend what the counselor said.

No →

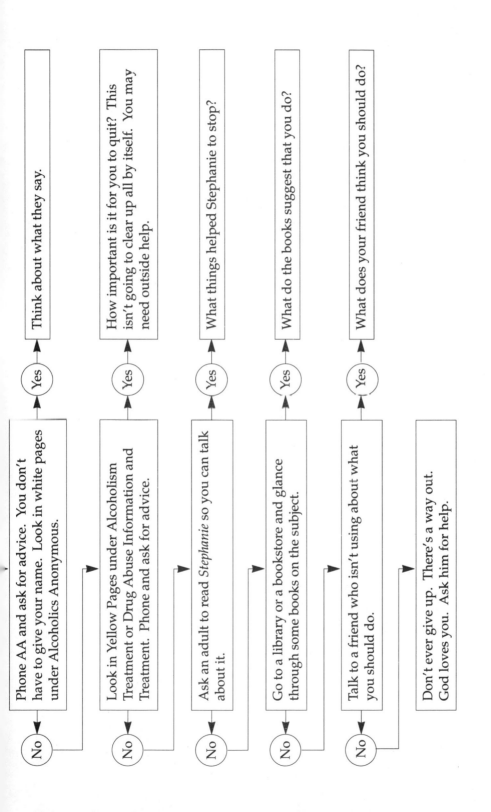

Phone AA and ask for advice. You don't have to give your name. Look in white pages under Alcoholics Anonymous.

Think about what they say.

Look in Yellow Pages under Alcoholism Treatment or Drug Abuse Information and Treatment. Phone and ask for advice.

How important is it for you to quit? This isn't going to clear up all by itself. You may need outside help.

Ask an adult to read *Stephanie* so you can talk about it.

What things helped Stephanie to stop?

Go to a library or a bookstore and glance through some books on the subject.

What do the books suggest that you do?

Talk to a friend who isn't using about what you should do.

What does your friend think you should do?

Don't ever give up. There's a way out. God loves you. Ask him for help.

Yes

No